CHERRY AMES,
COUNTRY DOCTOR'S NURSE

The CHERRY AMES *Stories*

☆   ☆   ☆

The VICKI BARR *Flight Stewardess Series*

Cherry followed Lois into the X-ray room

Cherry followed Lola into the X-ray room

CHERRY AMES COUNTRY DOCTOR'S NURSE

By

JULIE TATHAM

~~~~~~

NEW YORK

GROSSET & DUNLAP

Publishers

PRINTED IN THE UNITED STATES OF AMERICA

Contents

Contents

CHERRY AMES,
COUNTRY DOCTOR'S NURSE

~~~~~~~~~~~~~~~~~~~~~~~~~~~~~~~~~~

CHAPTER I

Reunion at No. 9

"ROMANCE?" CHERRY GRINNED AND RAN HER FINGERS through her dark curls. "I've forgotten the meaning of the word."

"That will be the day!" Redheaded Gwen Jones sniffed. "You're always involved in a mystery or a romance, and you know it, Cherry Ames."

"Or both," Mai Lee, the dainty Chinese-American nurse added with her sweet smile.

"Well, *I'm* never involved in anything exciting," Josie Franklin complained. "Romantic or otherwise."

Cherry chuckled, thinking that none of her classmates had changed a bit since they had entered Spencer Hospital's Nursing School as humble probationers. They were full-fledged R.N.'s now, but Gwen was just as slangy, Mai Lee was lovelier than ever, and Josie was still complaining about the lack of romance in her life.

The four young nurses were having brunch in the

living room of No. 9, their Greenwich Village apartment. Due to a round-robin letter started by Cherry, they had decided to have a Spencer Club reunion at their headquarters in New York City. Only four of the original members had been free to attend the reunion, but those four had had a wonderful week of indulging in the luxury of sleeping late, loafing, and talking about old times for hours on end.

Instead of eating at regular hours, they had brunch, high tea, and a late supper. "For just this one week," Josie had pleaded, "let's forget that we know all about calories and vitamins and minerals."

"Let's forget that we are nurses, period," Gwen had agreed emphatically. "I wouldn't have any other kind of career, but I don't want you other graduate nurses to threaten me with digestive disorders in my old age if I decide to exist for this one week on toasted English muffins and chocolate nut sundaes."

"I won't threaten you with anything," Mai Lee had chimed in, "because for once in my life I intend to gorge on pickled watermelon rind at every meal."

"Let's have this our motto"—Cherry summed it up— " 'What is one man's poison is another's meat.' "

They had determinedly and joyously lived up to this motto, but they frequently exchanged guilty glances when Bertha Larsen's name cropped up in their conversation. She was a wonderful cook and did not approve of meals which came straight from the delicatessen to the table.

"I'm almost glad Bertha couldn't tear herself away

from her Kentucky mountaineers," Gwen said over and over again. "And as for our married classmates, poor little Hausfraus! They probably had wholesome oatmeal for breakfast instead of this delicious pastrami for brunch."

On the last day of their vacation, Sunday, they decided to outdo themselves. "Like the convict's last meal before execution," Cherry said as she and Gwen made out the list. It was their turn to do the shopping, and they came back an hour later laden with big brown paper bags which they carried down the long hall to the dining room.

"The kitchenette's too small," Cherry explained cheerfully. "To save another trip we thought we might as well buy things for high tea and supper while we were there."

"Gracious!" Mai Lee gasped. "Did you buy everything in the delicatessen?"

"Just about," said Gwen, her blue eyes twinkling. "If you and Josie ever want to use this table again, we'll have to eat our way through this stuff."

"I think it looks very nice all cluttered," Cherry said complacently. "It's not really a dining room, anyway. Do you remember when we painted the furniture blue and lived in terror for fear the landlord would evict us?"

They all shuddered reminiscently and began to chat about the days when they had been visiting nurses, while Cherry and Gwen changed from street clothes into housecoats. Josie and Mai Lee were wearing short, quilted brunch coats over their pajamas, and in this becoming costume Mai Lee naturally looked more Chinese than ever. Josie looked unusually pretty too, Cherry thought, as they carried things into the living room which faced the street.

This room, with its gold-and-white wallpaper and gold gauze curtains, was the girls' pride and joy. Having little money to spend, they had worked hard to make it attractive—and it was. Sunlight streamed through the windows and logs crackled in the handsome fireplace. It was an Indian summer day in late October and really too warm for a fire but they had decided to have one, anyway, so that Josie and Mai Lee could toast muffins while Gwen and Cherry prepared the hot dishes in the tiny kitchenette.

"There's not room for both of us in here," Gwen said to Cherry as she dumped a package of frozen chicken livers into a frying pan of sizzling margarine. "Scram."

"Too bad about you," Cherry replied, cracking eggs into a bowl. "You can have your old chicken livers. I'm going to have a western omelet. Where is that large and luscious Bermuda onion we bought?"

"I have no idea," Gwen replied. "Josie probably put it in the refrigerator, thinking it was a grapefruit. Anything can happen when she's not wearing her glasses."

Cherry opened the door of the tiny icebox and promptly closed it. "Nothing," she said, "would induce me to poke around in that mess. I'm glad I'm leaving tomorrow at the crack of dawn."

"Selfish," said Gwen. "What's in the refrigerator,

anyway? Last time I opened it there was nothing but a stick of butter."

"That must have been when you arrived a week ago," Cherry said, laughing. "There's a little bit of everything in it now. We'd better send a wire to Bertha to come back and cope."

Gwen dumped the contents of the frying pan into a plate. "You can have the stove now. Lacking the courage to search for the onion, can you content yourself with plain scrambled eggs?"

"I guess I'll have to," Cherry said wistfully. "But I did crave a western omelet."

A few minutes later she joined the others in the living room and surveyed the dishes which they had set out on the long table in front of the sofa. "M-m-m, pickles, watermelon rind, salami, liverwurst, marmalade, grape jam, raspberry jelly—no, I find none of it very appealing."

Mai Lee handed her a toasted muffin on the end of a long fork. "Here, Cherry, this seems to have your name on it."

Cherry brightened. "Just the thing. I'll butter it and spread some garlic paste on it. We haven't had garlic bread since Friday."

"Oh, no!" Mai Lee and Josie cried in unison. "You can't."

"Why not?" Cherry demanded.

Mai Lee raised her eyes to the ceiling. "Garlic for brunch? How frightfully unladylike!"

"That's right," Josie added hastily. "Garlic in the

morning? Why, Cherry, how can you think of such a thing?"

Cherry's black eyes were wide with amazement. "What's come over you two? Since when did you get so refined?" She started off down the hall. "I'm going to get that garlic paste and have all I want of it."

Mai Lee's slim ivory hands closed around her wrists. "No, Cherry dear, you mustn't. I have decided to forego garlic today, so will the rest of you please be co-operative and forego it too?"

"I wouldn't touch a clove of it with a ten-foot pole," Josie said firmly. "Garlic and onions! Ugh!"

Cherry glared at her suspiciously. "Josie Franklin! Did you, by any chance, accidentally on purpose, mislay in our overcrowded refrigerator a large and lovely Bermuda onion which I bought this morning?"

Josie appealed to Mai Lee. "If I were going to fly back to my home town in Illinois tomorrow, I wouldn't eat any onions, would you, Mai Lee? Sure to make you airsick. Ver-ree airsick."

"Oh, absolutely," agreed Mai Lee.

"Me, airsick?" Gently but firmly Cherry freed herself from Mai Lee's grasp. "Now I know you're both crazy. Except for measles, mumps, and chicken pox, I've never been any kind of sick in my whole life. And in case you've forgotten what you learned in training about nutrition, onions and garlic are—"

"Very unromantic," Mai Lee finished for her. "The copilot of your plane is sure to be young and handsome. He'll come back sometime during the flight to Chicago for a cup of coffee, and when he sees you, he'll ask the stewardess to introduce you and—well, everything will be ruined if you reek of onions and garlic."

Cherry collapsed on the sofa. "That does it," she cried exasperatedly. "You're on the verge of a nervous breakdown, Mai Lee, and so is Josie. You'd better call up the registry right now and say that you can't take those private duty cases after all. You'd better turn yourselves into the nearest psychiatric ward."

Gwen, sitting cross-legged on the floor, interrupted with one of her puckish grins. "As a matter of fact, Ames," she said, "Josie and Mai Lee are making a lot of sense. All of us, except lucky you, have to report for duty tomorrow morning. So none of us had better reek of onions and garlic. Do you think it's fair for you to indulge when we can't?"

"Oh," Cherry cried contritely, "I never thought about that! I'm sorry, girls. Relaxing the way we all have this past week has made me selfish and inconsiderate. The sooner I get back into uniform the better. I wish," she finished unhappily, "that I were going on duty tomorrow morning too."

At that, they all began to comfort her at once:

"Cherry, darling, you couldn't be selfish or inconsiderate if you tried."

"If anyone deserves a vacation, it's you."

"You can have all the onions and garlic you like, but—"

"What I was trying to say was—"

Gwen finally silenced them with an upraised muffin.

"Cherry knows that so far as we're concerned she's like Caesar's wife—above reproach. What I strongly suspect is that she's involved in a romance right now and is keeping it a secret from us!"

"Romance?" Cherry grinned and ran her fingers through her dark curls. "I've forgotten the meaning of the word."

But she hadn't—not really. While the others chatted about their various beaux, she thought about two of the young men she had met during her nursing career, whom she had liked more than any of the others. They were ex-Captain Wade Cooper, now a pilot with Federal Airlines, and Dr. Marius Lexington Upham.

"Lex" had been an intern at Spencer Hospital when she was a senior nurse, and a recent note from him had told her that he was now Head Resident at a suburban hospital about forty miles from New York City.

"It's small compared with Spencer," Lex had written, "but it's very up-to-date, and the town, Sleepyside, is not at all sleepy. There's never a dull moment. With Election Day less than a month off, feeling is running high and I wouldn't be at all surprised if someone got murdered before the first Tuesday in November. This should intrigue you, Cherry, famous amateur detective that you are, although the murder will be purely political. What I'm driving at is this:

"Isn't it time you left Hilton and returned to the metropolitan area? Sleepyside is only an hour's drive from No. 9. There's a wonderful country doctor up here who needs a wonderful nurse like you. With

Thursday and Saturday afternoons and all day Sunday off every week, you'd have plenty of time for seeing your old friends. Especially your old and ever-loving friend, Lex."

Wade had written at about the same time to say that he was now on the New York–Mexico City run: "Your room at No. 9 has been vacant long enough. Why keep paying your share of the rent if you're never going to darken that blue doorway again? Answer: Get a job in or near the Big City and let me know when you're due to arrive so I can meet your plane with orchids and chocolate creams."

So along with the round-robin letter to her classmates, Cherry had sent post cards to Lex and Wade, saying that she planned to arrive in New York around the middle of October to spend a week at No. 9. "Strictly a girls' party," she wrote them both, "but do give me a ring if you have time."

Thinking back now, on the last day of her visit, Cherry wished that she hadn't sent those cards. She should have written them individual notes and sent them airmail with the definite date of her arrival. . . . Perhaps she shouldn't have written them at all! Just because they had written her recently didn't mean that they had meant what their letters implied. As old friends, they were just being polite. . . . They were both very attractive young men. . . . Wade probably was madly in love with a flight stewardess . . . Lex probably was engaged to a nurse.

Cherry squirmed inwardly. The week was almost

over and neither Wade nor Lex had called her! There was some excuse for Wade; planes didn't fly straight to Mexico City and right back again with the same personnel. Her card might well have arrived the day he took off and was still waiting for him at the Federal Airlines office . . . while *he* was basking in the beautiful climate of Mexico City during a stopover.

But Lex—there was no excuse for him! Even if he couldn't leave the hospital, he could have at least telephoned to say hello. Well, maybe the card got lost, Cherry reflected gloomily. Maybe she'd copied the address incorrectly. Thinking about it now she felt very confused. Had she sent the card to Sleepyside-on-Hudson, or to Sleepy Hollow, or, worse still, to Sunnyside, which, she knew, was the name of Washington Irving's home near Tarrytown? Washington Irving . . . *The Legend of Sleepy Hollow.* . . . "Oh, dear," she silently reproached herself. "I *am* confused. Why didn't I wait and telephone Lex and Wade after I got here?"

Josie's voice brought her out of her reverie. "Well, I *did* have a very nice beau once; at least Mai Lee said he liked me a lot. Do you girls remember Johnny Brent— the young doctor who was with me on several cases when I was a visiting nurse?"

"*I* remember him very well," said Gwen. "Unlike Cherry's beau, Wade Cooper, Johnny didn't mind dating the whole Spencer Club when he came to see you, Josie. A very nice guy, indeed. Have you heard from him recently, Josie?"

Josie shook her head mournfully. "I should have

dropped him a card to let him know that I was coming back to No. 9, but I didn't quite have the nerve."

"Lucky you," said Cherry enviously. "*I* did have the nerve to write both Wade *and* Lex that I'd be here for a week, and neither one of them has bothered to call. If anybody's a wallflower around here, I'm it!"

Gwen stared at her in amazement. "Why, that's not possible, Cherry. They're both madly in love with you. Why, even though Lex *thought* he was in love with somebody else when you were a flight nurse, you'll notice that he's still a bachelor. You sent him and Wade airmail letters of course?"

"Post cards," Cherry admitted regretfully. "The sad part of it is that when Lex wrote he hinted that he could get me what sounded like a fascinating job with a doctor whose office is only about an hour's drive from here." She covered her face with her hands. "I thought that Lex would call me as soon as I arrived and that we'd talk about it and—well, anyway, it's too late now."

"Oh, I give up!" Mai Lee exploded. "Keeping a secret can be more of a nuisance than fun." She knelt on the carpet at Cherry's feet. "I beg thy forgiveness, O Beauteous One! While you and Gwen were out marketing this morning, Lex called. He didn't get your card until late last night. Surprise! Surprise! I invited him for high tea this afternoon."

"Oh, *no!*" Josie screamed. "I must have been asleep when that happened."

"You were," said Mai Lee calmly. "I've been wondering why you were so co-operative about helping me keep Cherry away from garlic and onions. Do you sleep with one ear open?"

"You don't understand," Josie wailed. "You were out in the garden, Mai Lee, when Wade Cooper called from La Guardia. I invited *him* to high tea."

Cherry's scream was louder than Josie's had been. "Lex and Wade *both* here for tea? Oh, I can't face it!"

"Neither can I!" Gwen shrieked. "They'll fight a duel with cream puffs at twenty paces. Our bee-you-tee-ful apartment will be ruined. Utterly ruined!"

Cherry slid off the sofa to join the others on the carpet. Stretched out full length, her arms folded on her chest, she fluttered her curly black lashes and pretended to faint dead away.

~~~~~~

CHAPTER II

A Change of Plans

"DON'T LIE THERE PLAYING POSSUM, AMES," GWEN snorted derisively. "If your cheeks were pale, I'd check your pulse and respiration. But since they're redder than the roses on your housecoat, you fail to arouse my sympathy." She nudged Cherry with her bare toes. "Arise, Lily Maid of Astolat. There's work to be done."

Cherry moaned feebly. "I know. Wade and Lex probably think high tea begins at four on the dot. It's long past high noon now. I've got to get glamorous, and ditto for the apartment. We haven't given it more than a lick and a promise all week."

Mai Lee smiled. "There's an old poem which covers this situation. I think John Gay wrote it, but I can only remember one verse:

"'How happy could I be with either,
Were t'other dear charmer away!
But while ye thus tease me together,
To neither a word will I say!'"

Gwen clapped her hands. "That *is* the answer. Cherry can just play dumb. Beautiful but dumb."

Cherry groaned and fluttered her lashes again. "I'm not going to play anything. I'm not going to be here. I'm going back into training. The only place I'd feel safe would be in a 'Beaux Parlor' with a lot of student nurses and their dates."

It was Mai Lee's turn to applaud. "That's the real answer of course. There's safety in numbers. We'll turn the tea into a tea party."

"Oh, fine," Josie jeered. "You and Gwen can have the Mad Hatter and the March Hare for your dates. That leaves me with the Dormouse."

Cherry sat up suddenly. "Don't be silly, Josie. We'll ask Johnny Brent. I'll invite him myself if you feel shy about it." Scrambling to her feet she raced off toward the phone, adding over one shoulder, "After all, Josie, it's the least I can do since I have *you* to thank for Wade."

When she came back a few minutes later she said: "He accepts with pleasure, Josie. He's dying to see you." Cherry glared at Gwen. "Do something about getting yourself a date. We only need one more man to make it an eightsome."

Gwen glared right back. "I can't produce a white rabbit without a tall silk hat. Have you got one, wizard?"

"Let's leave hats and rabbits out of this conversation," Cherry retorted. "How about that boy you went to school with in your home town, Gwen? Ben Taylor— his family's still living in New York."

Gwen sighed. "How unromantic can I get? Oh, all right, I'll invite good old lanky sandy-haired Ben."

"He's very nice—and nice-looking too," Cherry said crisply. "I'm going to spend all my time with him while you and Mai Lee entertain Wade and Lex."

"Oh, make some sense for a change!" Gwen departed for the phone.

The others were carrying the brunch things back to the kitchenette when Gwen shouted to them from the hall:

"Ben, too, accepts with pleasure. I'll do the dishes, since my lovely manicure would be wasted on him."

"You'll do nothing of the sort!" Cherry yelled back. "I'll do the dishes and you can give me a manicure afterward."

They met in the dining room and hugged each other affectionately. "If only you were twins," Gwen said fondly, "you'd be the belles of the ball, so you must be glamorous at all costs."

"I am a twin," Cherry reminded her with a giggle.

"I mean girl twins," Gwen retorted. "Identical girl twins. That brother of yours is as blond as you are dark, but I wish Charlie were here. At least I didn't go to school with *him*."

"Well, I did," Cherry replied tartly.

Giggling and getting into one another's way, they somehow managed to get the apartment into a gleaming state of tidiness. Mai Lee filled the vases with chrysanthemums from the little garden, and they all took turns taking showers. Then they donned their best afternoon frocks, but at the last minute Cherry decided to wear the royal-blue gabardine suit which she had bought on one of their many shopping trips.

"Simply because it's brand new," she told Gwen.

"And also very becoming." Gwen grinned at Cherry's reflection in the mirror of the room they shared. "Furthermore, as you are fully aware, it will be just right if one or both of your beaux asks you to have dinner with him. Which they will."

Cherry ran a comb through her damp, dark curls. "Which they won't. Nobody could eat dinner after one of our high teas, and Lex probably will have to go right back to the hospital. And Wade—"

The doorbell rang. "Y-you-you answer it, Gwen," Cherry begged. "I-I c-can't. It might be b-both of them."

Gwen tossed her red hair. "Fiddle-de-dee. Or do I mean Tweedledum and Tweedledee? If Mai Lee can quote poetry at crucial moments, I guess I can." And she did:

> " 'Tweedledum and Tweedledee
>   Agreed to have a battle;
> For Tweedledum said Tweedledee
>   Had spoiled his nice new rattle.
>
> " 'Just then flew down a monstrous crow,
>   As black as a tar barrel;
> Which frightened both the heroes so,
>   They quite forgot their quarrel.' "

"All we need is a black crow," Gwen finished as the bell rang again. "There's a crazy artist three gardens away who keeps one as a pet. Shall I go and get it?"

From their bedroom Mai Lee and Josie howled subduedly:

"Won't somebody please answer the door? We're not dressed."

"Do as you're told," Cherry commanded Gwen desperately.

"Now don't you wish you were twin girls?" Gwen replied.

"No, I wish I were the Unicorn!" Cherry sailed past her and answered the door herself.

It was Wade, looking taller and tanner than ever as he sandwiched her hand in both of his and said:

"Cherry! You look good enough to eat."

Cherry winced slightly and freed her hand. "It's grand to see you, Wade. If you're hungry, come right into our parlor where we have a feast fit for a king waiting for you."

He followed her into the living room, chuckling. "I didn't mean that I was starving for *food*. Speaking of which, I have a bone to pick with you."

"Oh, oh," Cherry thought, "he's in one of his possessive moods. What'll I do if Lex is in the same sort of mood?" Demurely she sat on the edge of the sofa and he promptly sat beside her. "We haven't any bones for you to pick," she said, "but there are tons of sandwiches. Help yourself."

He ignored her and said accusingly, "You were out

in Arizona not long ago, working on a dude ranch, and you never even called me up. Did you forget that Tucson is my home town?"

Cherry smiled, regaining her poise. Wade *was* a Tweedledum, just a great big schoolboy who would never quite grow up. She was glad of that, and liked him more than ever. "I thought of you all the time I was in Tucson," she told him, "but I did remember that you had given up your auto-repair shop there and had gone back to flying. Once a pilot, always a pilot, I guess; just like once a nurse, always a nurse. Except," she added ruefully, "I don't seem to have a job at the moment."

"Great!" he cried enthusiastically. "When I found your card waiting for me at the office this morning, I died a thousand deaths thinking that maybe you'd already come and gone off on another cruise to the Caribbean. Couldn't you have sent a telegram instead of a post card?" he added reprovingly. "I got in last night but didn't bother to pick up my mail until this morning. A telegram would have been forwarded." Suddenly he stared at her with tender concern. "Cherry! Do you mean that you've been out of work so long that you're —you're broke? You could only *afford* a post card?"

Cherry swayed back against the cushions, weak with laughter. "No, no, Wade. I've plenty of jobs waiting for me in my own home town: in the clinic, the hospital, and the new rest home. It was silly of me not to write you an airmail letter, but you see I was sort of planning on getting a job in a New York suburb—"

The bell rang again, imperiously, and Cherry knew that it must be impatient Lex who had jabbed the button in that commanding manner. She was grateful to hear from a rustle of taffeta and a sardonic cough that Gwen was answering it.

In a minute Gwen ushered in Lex, and dropping a low curtsy in front of Cherry, she said: "Your highness, may I present his lordship, the human tornado, the brilliant, unpredictable Dr. Marius Lexington Upham!"

Wade immediately stood up, glowering, and Cherry knew that Gwen was right. The only thing to do was to make a comedy of the whole situation. She arose majestically and with a queenly gesture extended one hand to Lex, praying that he was in one of his humorous moods.

He was, thank goodness! Bowing low, he kissed Cherry's hand, and said to Wade out of the corner of his mouth:

"Captain Cooper, I believe."

Wade grinned broadly and the two young men shook hands very amicably. Mai Lee and Josie appeared then, and shortly afterward Dr. Johnny Brent and Ben Taylor arrived. Ben lavishly admired the flowers and refused to believe that they had been grown in a city garden, so Mai Lee took him out to their back yard to show him what wonders she wrought there.

Gwen attached herself to Lex, chatting vivaciously about old times at Spencer, and Josie and Johnny joined them to form a group—a very medical group, Cherry reflected a bit enviously. Air-minded Wade was frantically trying to hold her attention, but his technical conversation about engines was over her head. Finally she got a word in edgewise:

"Tell me about Mexico City, Wade," she pleaded. "I hear that it has the most perfect climate in the world."

This started Wade off again on another tangent, but Cherry listened only halfheartedly. She realized suddenly that, although he was one of the nicest young men she had ever met, her real interests lay with the medical profession. A week away from it had been long enough; she longed to get back into uniform. Out of the corner of one eye she glanced at Lex. He was wearing a tweed suit very much like the one that Wade was wearing, but she was sure that even if she had never met him before she would have known that he was a doctor. There was something so intelligent about his face, and his golden-brown eyes under those decided dark brows were so alert. Every strand of his straight sandy hair was as smoothly in place as Wade's brown hair was rumpled.

Their eyes met for a moment and Cherry knew that he had read her mind. She *was* very much interested in hearing more about the job he had hinted at in his last letter. She didn't really have to fly back to Hilton tomorrow. There was no place like home, of course, but an assignment in a New York suburb seemed awfully enticing because of its proximity to No. 9—and more especially, because Lex had written that there was never a dull moment there. Cherry wasn't quite sure what he had meant by "a political murder" but she was intrigued.

"—and I'll bring you back a *rebozo*," Wade was saying. "A salmon-pink one would be very becoming."

Cherry pulled herself together, although she had no idea what a rebozo was, and said, "That would be lovely, Wade."

He stood up. "Well, I've got to scram back to the airport now." He said good-by to the others, and Cherry went with him to the door. "Don't you dare leave tomorrow," he admonished her. "Remember, I've got a whole three-day week end coming to me soon. We'll do the town together as of yore."

Cherry quickly made up her mind. "Wade, I have a reservation with Federal for Flight 66 to Chicago tomorrow morning. Will you cancel it for me?"

"Can do." He gave her a swift brotherly hug and strode off down the hall.

Cherry went back into the living room where she was immediately drawn into the medical group which now included Mai Lee and Ben.

"It's all settled," Lex said in that commanding, impatient way of his. "You start to work tomorrow morning, Cherry, for Dr. Clem."

"That's right," Gwen added. "With Saturday afternoons and Sundays off, same as we do, we can have a Spencer Club reunion every week end."

"You'll adore Dr. Clem," Josie was saying. "He sounds like a great big lovable Teddy bear."

Lex howled with laughter. "That's just an act he puts

on! He's one of the smartest general practitioners in the county, but whenever it suits his purposes he pretends to be dim-witted and slowed down by age, although he's still in his early fifties."

"What *I* like best about him," Gwen continued, "is that he's just as interested in his patients' emotional and financial problems as he is in their physical problems. You're going to love your Dr. Clem, Cherry."

Cherry gasped. *"My* Dr. Clem?"

Nobody paid any attention to her, and Josie said to young Dr. Brent, "Cherry will love working for him, won't she, Johnny?"

Dr. Brent nodded. "I'd love to work for him myself. I wish he needed a bright young assistant."

Lex grinned. "That could easily be arranged. The M.D.'s in Sleepyside would welcome you with open arms, Johnny. Up there, we're suffering from a shortage of doctors *and* nurses." He took Cherry's hand and said soberly, "Dr. Clem needs a nurse like you, not only because of your experience but because you're so flexible. He spends more time in his patients' homes than he does in his office. He tries to help them with all of their problems and will expect you to do the same. That, if nothing else, should make you accept the job."

Cherry glowed. She did love to help people solve their problems! Early in her training she had learned that this was an important part of a nurse's duties. Worries of all kinds kept sick people from getting well and no good doctor or nurse overlooked this factor in the treatment.

"It's all settled," Lex said. "You start to work tomorrow
for Dr. Clem."

"I'd like to work for Dr. Clem," she said, "but could I qualify? I haven't had any secretarial experience, and I've forgotten what little bookkeeping I learned in high school."

Lex gave her hand a reassuring pat. "The secretarial part of your job will be the least of your worries. Lola Wright can explain it all to you in an hour or so."

"Lola Wright?" Cherry asked curiously.

"That's right, Wright," Lex said with a chuckle. "Lola has been Dr. Clem's nurse for the past twenty years and she wants to retire now. She's been invited by old friends to drive to Florida with them if she can leave early on Tuesday morning. That's why you have to start tomorrow morning, Cherry. But don't worry. Lola will spend the whole first day with you showing you the ropes. Come on. Get ready so we can drive up this evening."

"She's practically packed already," Gwen pointed out.

"Packed?" Cherry wailed. "All of my uniforms are home."

"I'll lend you some of mine," the girls offered in one voice. Gwen gave Cherry a little push. "Call your mother right now. If she sends your uniforms off tomorrow, they'll arrive in time for you to bring ours back next Sunday."

Almost before she knew it, Cherry was talking to her mother, breathlessly explaining her last-minute change in plans.

"It sounds like a job that will suit you to a T," Mrs.

Ames said in her gay, youthful voice. "I'll pack your uniforms right away. Where will you be staying in Sleepyside, dear?"

"Oh, my goodness," Cherry gasped, "I don't know! But Lex is right here. I'll ask him."

"With Miss Marcia Charlton," Lex said in answer to her question. "She runs—what I guess you'd call—a very refined boardinghouse on Main Street. I made a tentative reservation for you with the housekeeper this morning."

Cherry relayed her new address to her mother, and after promising to write soon, hung up. Then she asked Lex:

"How can we make sure that Miss Charlton has a vacant room, and even if she has, maybe she won't think me refined enough to be a boarder?"

He laughed, took the phone from its cradle, and dialed long-distance. After giving the operator a Sleepyside number, he said to Cherry, "Just to make sure that Miss Marcia does have a room, because it's the only place in town where you could stay. And, by the way, the reason why I didn't get your card until last night was because you addressed it to Sleepy Hollow, which happens to be a valley, not a town." Suddenly his joking attitude changed.

Crisp with dignity he said into the mouthpiece, "Good evening, Miss Charlton. Dr. Upham speaking. How are you? . . . I'm glad to hear it. I'm calling about a room for the nurse I'm bringing up from the city to take Miss Lola Wright's place. . . . Yes, that is right. . . . Miss Cherry Ames, the daughter of Mr. and Mrs. William Ames, of Hilton, Illinois. . . . No, he hasn't met her yet, but Miss Ames is an old friend of mine, so you can take my word— . . . Very well, very well. But you will hold the room until eleven? . . . Thank you very much."

He hung up, shaking his head ruefully. "Wow! What a stickler for formalities she is! Flatly refused to take you in until Dr. Clem has definitely approved of you."

"Quite right of her," Cherry said, feeling rather nervous. "So I'm not going up tonight. If Dr. Clem doesn't approve of me, I'd have to come right back by train, something I don't relish doing late at night. Oh, why did I cancel my plane reservation? I just feel in my bones that Dr. Clem *won't* approve of me."

"Don't be silly," Lex said. "I ran into him this morning at the hospital and told him all about you. He wants you so much that he made me promise to kidnap you if you didn't come of your own free will."

"That I don't believe," Cherry said emphatically. "And how can we be sure that he will be able to interview me this evening? Suppose he's out on call when we arrive and doesn't get back until *after* eleven?"

"That would be most unfortunate," Lex agreed, "because Miss Marcia won't allow anyone to enter the sacred portals of The Manor after 11 P.M. Even guests who have occupied suites there since she converted the old family mansion into a boardinghouse have to obey that rule. But have no fears, little one," he added soothingly, "if we miss Dr. Clem, I'll admit you into the hospital as a patient so you can have a place to lay your weary head. M-m-m. Now let's see. With those rosy cheeks you'd certainly get into the isolation ward as a scarlet-fever case."

Cherry relaxed, laughing. Good old Lex! He was forever teasing her, but she knew that no matter what happened he would take care of her. Half an hour later he heaved her suitcase into the back of his old but shiny-clean roadster and helped her into the front seat. It seemed like a lark then with Gwen, Josie, and Mai Lee waving good-bys from the stoop of No. 9. But when they turned up into the broad West Side Highway, her misgivings came back.

Dr. Clem probably would turn her down. Lex, undoubtedly, had exaggerated her good points and mentioned none of her faults. Dr. Clem was used to an older nurse who had been with him for almost a quarter of a century. He would take one look at Cherry Ames and pronounce her a flibbertigibbet. Oh, why hadn't she stuck to her original plans? Why was she forever doing impulsive, foolish things?

Cherry stared unseeingly across the black waters of the Hudson River at the twinkling lights on the New Jersey shore. She tried desperately to think of her good points, but all of the pictures on her own personal mental television set showed her only as getting into scrapes and frantically getting out of them.

Suddenly it didn't seem like a lark any more—it seemed like a wild-goose chase.

CHAPTER III

Cherry Meets the Mayor

WHEN THEY LEFT THE CITY BEHIND THEM AND TURNED into the broad four-lane parkway, Cherry's spirits began to rise. She couldn't feel depressed long when she knew she was starting out on what might well turn out to be another exciting adventure. She hadn't been listening very attentively to Lex's conversation after they left No. 9, but now he said something which made her sit up straight:

"So you can see what I meant when I wrote you that I suspect a political murder will be committed soon."

"Political murder," she repeated wonderingly. "Just what do you mean by that, Lex? Political intrigues baffle me."

He turned his head slightly to grin at her. "I know just how you feel. Politics always used to be beyond me, but when you're living in a small town like Sleepyside you can't escape them. As Dr. Clem's nurse you'll find

28

yourself involved in one of the two warring factions before long, so you may as well get a clear picture of the situation right now. Let's start with the two main characters—the candidates in the mayoralty campaign. Cy Hillman has been our mayor for the past twenty years and he naturally expects to be re-elected next month. At least he took re-election for granted until young Harry Jenner appeared on the scene. Harry is a brilliant lawyer and so attractive in a firebrand sort of way that I'm not at all sure that I want you to meet him. In fact, I'm green with jealousy just thinking about it."

Cherry laughed, and using one of Lex's pet expressions, she said, "Have no fears, little one. I probably won't meet him unless he gets sick or hurt and comes to Dr. Clem for treatment."

"I doubt if he'll get sick," Lex said in a strangely sober voice, "but he might get hurt. Accidents can happen in a political campaign like this—oh, I don't mean that," he interrupted himself. "Let's begin at the beginning again. According to the *Sleepyside Sun,* both men are local lads; they were born in Sleepyside, and after graduating from high school, went off to college and law school. Cy, of course, who's in his sixties, is old enough to be Harry's father. I gather that he, Cy, got a job with a Chicago law firm after being admitted to the bar, but about twenty-five years ago he came back to Sleepyside, preferring, I guess, to be a big frog in a little pond. Anyway, he invested his savings in real estate and, politically speaking, got to be a big frog very fast, climbing rapidly from town councilman to supervisor to mayor, which office he's held ever since."

"Well, he must be a good mayor," Cherry put in, "otherwise, he—"

"Oh, he's a good mayor all right," Lex interrupted, "but I'm beginning to think that he's not the People's Choice—not the Little People's Choice, anyway, which Harry Jenner definitely is. Harry was admitted to the bar about eighteen months ago, came right back to Sleepyside, and hung out his shingle. That's when I received the Residency at the hospital, and the town was already in a political uproar because the pros and cons of a new grade school were being argued heatedly and heavily. At the last referendum four years ago, the vote was an overwhelming No, though it was obvious to everyone with eyes in his head that we need not one new school, but two. However, such things have always been controlled by the powerful minority, which consists of big landowners who have no young children and who always get out and vote against anything which will increase their taxes. When the referendum came up again, Harry Jenner realized that the Little People could win if only *they'd* get out and vote. This he accomplished through fiery speeches, a door-to-door campaign, and impassioned open letters to the *Sun* which were printed on the front page."

"Good for Harry Jenner," Cherry said. "I like him already."

"So do I," Lex admitted, "but half of the town doesn't. Those who are glad that we're at long last going to have a new school are solidly behind him and they nominated him for mayor. But we are the weak majority."

"I don't understand," Cherry complained. "The word 'majority' has always meant power to me."

"You're wrong, honey chile," Lex said in that condescending way of his. "The majority of people, through ignorance or laziness, never get around to registering, so they can't vote on Election Day. You don't necessarily have to be a registered voter in order to cast your ballot at a referendum. If everybody who voted in favor of the new school could vote for Harry in November, he'd probably win. But as it is, he hasn't got a chance. The old-timers—the big landowners, who can and will vote—will defeat him in a walk."

"Maybe that's just as well," said Cherry thoughtfully. "How can you be sure that a man as young as Harry Jenner will make a good mayor?"

Lex shrugged. "That's another point in Cy's favor. Right now I think that Harry is just exactly what Sleepyside needs to wake it up. But suppose he turns out to be nothing but a new broom sweeping clean? He might inaugurate a lot of much-needed improvements in the various departments, but there's a good chance that while sweeping clean he'll antagonize the old-timers who are really the backbone of the town. Without their support, I'm afraid Sleepyside will collapse into utter chaos."

"Well," Cherry said stanchly, "I don't think much of your old-timers if they voted against the new school.

They couldn't have the real interests of the town at heart. A new grade school was recently built in Hilton. Mother and Dad and Dr. Joe campaigned for it, although they're taxpayers with no young children. Why aren't the Sleepyside old-timers like that?"

They turned off the parkway and traveled westward through a tiny hamlet to turn north again into a two-lane macadam road.

"This is the Albany Post Road," Lex said. "We're almost there. I think—" The rest of his remark was drowned out by the roar of an express train as it thundered past, cutting off Cherry's view of the river.

"I think," Lex repeated, when quiet reigned again, "that you should reserve judgment until you meet some of the old-timers like Dr. Clem and Miss Marcia."

"Were they against the new school?" Cherry asked in amazement.

"No," Lex said, "although since the polling is secret, nobody knows how they voted on the referendum, but they've made no bones about the fact that they're going to vote for Cy in the coming election. It's not as simple as it sounds, Cherry. There's such a thing as loyalty which influences people—people like Dr. Clem and Miss Marcia who have known Cy all of their lives. From where they sit he's been a good mayor for twenty years. Harry Jenner is nothing but an upstart—an infant tyro, in their opinion, and I'm not at all sure that they're not right to campaign against him. For one thing, his platform includes spending a sizable sum improving town-owned tenements, which apparently

don't need improvements. The mayor claims that if
Harry gets in he'll give the contracts to pals of his to
repay them for working to get him elected. He further
claims that if these 'frills,' as he calls them, are added,
the rents will have to be hiked beyond the means of
the present tenants. And so the people who live in those
tenements down by the water front will have no place
to go."

"Which one do you believe is speaking the truth?"
Cherry asked. "The mayor or Harry Jenner?"

"I am forced to believe the mayor," Lex replied.
"After all, he is the head of the committee which op-
erates the buildings. They were taken over in lieu of
back taxes many years ago, and although it's rather unusual for a town to act in the capacity of a landlord, the
very fact that it has become a community project makes
me feel sure that Harry's Face-Lift-the-Tenements platform is a purely political maneuver."

"I don't understand," Cherry complained.

"I mean," Lex explained, "that Harry emphasizes
that angle in his campaign speeches with the hope that
it will encourage poor people to get out and vote for
him. Also, it is perfectly conceivable that he has, as the
mayor implies, made a private deal with a big, influential contractor. That kind of thing is done all the time
during electioneering."

Cherry thought for a minute. "The mayor must be
speaking the truth. In Hilton, anyway, landlords are
forced by law to keep their buildings in good shape.
Even the cheapest cold-water flats are inspected regu-

larly by public-health and fire officials. I'm sure about this. Dad's a real-estate man, you know."

"We have the same laws in Sleepyside," Lex agreed, "and so far as I know they are enforced. I wouldn't say that the tenements are things of beauty, but the exteriors give no indication that they are the health and fire hazards Harry Jenner claims they are. I've never been inside one, so I don't know."

"That's a high and mighty resident for you," Cherry said with a sniff. "If you were an intern riding the ambulance you would know. But there must be patients in the ward and the clinic who live in those tenements."

"There are," Lex admitted, "but I've never heard one of them complain about his dwelling place. Furthermore, a large sum of money is allocated annually from town funds for the very purpose of maintaining those buildings, and the rents received are reinvested in the property in the form of improvements. When the town decided to become a landlord, the whole idea was to own and operate a model low-rent project for the benefit of the poor. So I must conclude that those tenements are in A-1 shape with all modern improvements."

"In other words," Cherry summed it up, "you think that Harry Jenner's Face-Lift-the-Tenements platform is part of a mudslinging campaign?"

Lex hesitated. "I know and like the guy, so I won't go that far, but by implication he is accusing the housing committee, which is headed by the mayor, of misappropriation of town funds. What I really think is what I said before. If he gets into office he'll be a new broom sweeping clean a lot of things that don't need sweeping. And I am not the only one who feels that way about Harry. All of the old-timers, who felt that the little red schoolhouse was good enough for them, feel that face lifting the tenements comes under the heading of unnecessary and expensive glamorization. Then there are others, like Dr. Clem, who came out for the new school due to Harry's efforts, but who frown upon his Face-Lift-the-Tenements platform. Miss Marcia is another one, and I assure you that both she and Dr. Clem really do have the interests of the town at heart. Why, the town grew up around their ancestral estates! Her home is at one end of Main Street and his is at the other. Both families date back to pre-Revolution days. The Charltons were lords of the manor and Dr. Clem's ancestors were rich tenant farmers. During the war for our independence, this part of the state was known as the Neutral Ground." Lex shook his head. "Nobody was very neutral and the land was constantly ravished. Most of the Charltons were Royalists and after the war a great deal of their land was confiscated by the state and divided among the tenant farmers who fought on the side of the Colonists." He chuckled. "I guess the feud dates back to then."

"Feud?" Cherry groaned. "I got mixed up in one of those when I was a mountaineer nurse in Kentucky with Bertha. What have I got myself into this time? Political murder and a feud! Who is feuding with whom?"

Lex's chuckle became a roar of laughter. "I guess I am painting a rather lurid picture for you. All I know about a feud is that Miss Marcia and Dr. Clem don't speak. This sometimes creates unbelievably funny situations. They're both very civic-minded and so are thrown together a lot at various town meetings. If they wish to converse they do it through a third person, who is usually poor Lola."

"Now you tell me!" Cherry gasped in mock dismay. "Do I have to attend those meetings and act as middleman—I mean, middlewoman?"

"Oh, sure," Lex said easily. "And you'll love it. You'll also fall in love with Dr. Clem at first sight, and vice versa. And, as a matter of fact, I think eventually you'll grow fond of Miss Marcia, though I may as well warn you right now, don't pull any of your usual pranks at The Manor or you'll find yourself out on the street."

"Pranks," Cherry said with a sniff. "I haven't indulged in one since I earned my cap. Well, not many, anyway," she finished with a giggle. "Tell me more about Miss Marcia. I'm scared to death of her already."

"I don't know much," Lex admitted. "Rumor hath that she was once as young and gay and beautiful as you, but that's hard to believe, except on the rare occasions when her mask slips. She limps slightly as the result of an accident which happened so long ago that even Lola Wright doesn't know anything about it. Dr. Clem probably would know, but of course he never mentions Miss Marcia's name."

"What did you mean about her mask slipping occasionally?" Cherry asked curiously.

"You'll see for yourself," Lex replied mysteriously. "It's hard to explain, but every now and then I get the impression that she isn't as grim as she pretends to be. Once, it was the ghost of a smile. Another time, it seemed to me that she was trying so hard not to cry that —well, anyway, here we are." He slowed, turned off to the right, and stopped. "This is Dr. Clem's end of Main Street and, as you can see, his house is right smack on the corner of the main highway which was once the Old Albany Post Road. A lovely house, but pretty incongruous at this spot, isn't it?"

Cherry stared at the simple, oblong-shaped white frame house which looked as though it should have been set well back from a country road with trees, shrubs, and perhaps a brook running in between. But instead, right across the street was a modern diner with neon lights which proclaimed that it was the SLEEPY-SIDE COFFEE SHOP. Beyond it was a drugstore, and beyond that was another neon sign announcing the title of the movie which was playing at the Cameo Theater.

"It certainly is incongruous," Cherry agreed. "We haven't got lovely colonial farmhouses like that in Hilton. If we did, there'd be a vegetable garden in the back and a cowshed and a chicken coop, and Dr. Clem would keep a goat and ducks and geese." She jumped out of the car and peered into the semidarkness cast by the shadow of the street lamp on the corner. "Why, there's nothing there but a garage."

"That's right." Lex joined her on the sidewalk. "When Dr. Clem was a boy, several acres of farmland sloped away from the back of the house. But his parents sold it piecemeal, so that he could go to college and medical school. All that's left is this small plot of land." He tucked her hand through the crook of his arm. "Come on! I'm dying to have you meet him. He's still a country bumpkin at heart, but wait until you see what he's done to the ground floor of his house. Wow! It's the most modern doctor's office around here, complete with rubber-tiled floors, picture windows, Venetian blinds, and last but not least, a lab that is the envy of our hospital."

A neat red-brick path led from the sidewalk to the front steps, and on one side of the path was the wooden silhouette of a large gray squirrel whose body proudly bore the illuminated legend:

CLEMUEL BROWN, M.D.
Office Hours: 10–12 A.M.
6–8 P.M.

"A gift from a patient," Lex explained. "And you might say the same about the renovated ground floor. Poor Dr. Clem! His patients rarely pay him in cash. But it seems to work out very well. His lawns are manicured in the summer, his flower borders are the envy of the garden club, the path is shoveled during the winter snows, the outside of the house is painted every year, the roof never lacks a shingle, and as for his ancient car, so many mechanics fight for the privilege of servicing it, I doubt if it'll ever wear out. So you can see what I mean about the bookkeeping end of your job. It's practically nil, since with a few exceptions, it's based on the barter system."

Cherry nodded understandingly. "Dr. Joe's practice was like that until he gave it up in order to devote himself to experimental work in his laboratory. It was he, you know, who first made me take an interest in biology and chemistry when I was in high school. He taught me an awful lot, which made the courses we had in training much easier, too. At the moment I can't remember anything, though I did take a refresher course at the Hilton Clinic in general lab work not long ago."

"Don't worry," Lex reassured her. "It'll all come back tomorrow while Lola's showing you the ropes."

They climbed the steps to the narrow stoop which was covered by a sloping portion of the green roof. There was a small light above the door, illuminating a sign which said:

"Back at 10 P.M."

Cherry glanced at her wrist watch. "Oh, dear! We'll have to wait an hour."

"So what?" Lex whirled her around. "In spite of your lavish high tea I'm starving, and I'll bet you are too. I wish it weren't Sunday, so we could go some place to dance. But the food's good at the coffee shop and the coffee even better."

Once they were inside the diner and seated on stools

at the long, white-topped counter, Cherry realized that she was hungry. Taped to the mirror on the wall facing her was a list of SPECIALS and she immediately decided on the beef stew, explaining to Lex:

"It's about time I got back into the routine of eating sensibly. I'm glad now the girls wouldn't let me have garlic and onions for brunch. Little did I know, then, that I was going to be interviewed by Dr. Clem this evening."

"Ben," Lex said to the man behind the counter, "this is Miss Cherry Ames. She's going to take Lola Wright's place. Ben," he told Cherry, "is the owner of the coffee shop, and his wife is one of Dr. Clem's favorite patients."

Cherry and Ben shook hands, then Lex said, "We'll both have the beef stew, please." He slid off the stool, jingling the change in his pocket, and wandered off toward the juke box in the rear. "Let's have some music while we eat."

Cherry realized then that the "diner" part of this restaurant was really only a front. A small flight of stairs just beyond the counter showed that it was a two-story house and she guessed that Mr. and Mrs. Ben lived on the floor above. She tucked her gloves into her handbag and her eyes wandered back to the mirror. Then she noticed for the first time that there was a man in the booth directly behind her. Only his head, shoulders, and forearms were reflected in the mirror. He was drinking coffee as he read a newspaper which was spread out on the table. Suddenly his face became con-

Cherry snatched up the crumpled ball of newspaper

torted with rage and his hand shook, so that the coffee slopped over the rim of the cup as he put it back in the saucer. Then he sank back into the booth and all she could see was his hands: two large thick-fingered hands that ripped the front page from the newspaper and wadded it into a ball. To Cherry's amazement, this ball was suddenly hurled out of the booth to land beneath her heels which were hooked over the rungs of her stool.

"My goodness," she thought, "that man is mad in both senses of the word. Why on earth would he want to pelt me?" Then it dawned on her that he had no way of knowing that she had been watching his reflection in the mirror. She also had the uncanny feeling that if he did know she had been watching his angry gestures he would be even more angry than he was now.

Overcome by curiosity, Cherry slid off the stool, snatched up the crumpled ball of newspaper, and slipped it into her handbag just as Lex came waltzing back to the tune of the "Blue Danube."

"Do you love this one as much as you used to?" he asked softly.

"It will always be my favorite waltz," Cherry replied, and hitched herself back on the stool as Ben appeared with their stew. Instead of chatting between mouthfuls, Cherry kept her eyes glued to the mirror for signs of life in the booth behind her. But there was nothing, for even the pudgy fingers had disappeared. And she knew that if she told Lex what had happened he would only scold her with the old refrain:

"Curiosity killed the cat" or "Must you always let your imagination run away with you?"

The very emptiness of that booth made Cherry feel that perhaps she *had* imagined the whole thing. And then the man emerged. Without turning her head, Cherry could see that he was of medium height with heavy shoulders and was very well dressed. What amazed her was that the expression on his face was that of complete geniality. And yet it was the same man— she was sure of it.

Moving with light, graceful steps he laid a bill beside the cash register and said, "I guess that covers it, Ben." Then, catching sight of Lex, he extended his hand. "Good evening, Dr. Upham. How are things at the hospital?"

"Fine," Lex said as they shook hands. Turning to Cherry, he added, "Miss Ames, may I present our mayor, the Honorable Cyrus Hillman?"

CHAPTER IV

Dr. Clem

CHERRY ALMOST FELL OFF HER STOOL WITH SURPRISE. She forced herself to smile at the mayor but she couldn't make herself shake hands with him. Only a few minutes ago those pudgy, manicured fingers had angrily crushed a sheet of newspaper into a ball, and that smiling face had been contorted with rage.

"Miss Ames," Lex was saying, "is going to be Dr. Clem's new nurse."

"Indeed?" The mayor bowed graciously. "Welcome to Sleepyside, Miss Ames. I am sure that you will be a most valuable—as well as a most decorative—addition to our community."

"Thank you." Cherry tried desperately to put some warmth into her voice. Could this charming man be the same one she had watched in the mirror, or had the mirror played tricks on her?

With another bow, he took his hat from the rack near the door and disappeared into the street.

44

"Well, what do you think of our Cy?" Lex asked.

"He's very attractive," Cherry said, and added with a teasing grin, "You're going to be just as handsome when your hair and eyebrows turn white. Is the mayor like you in other ways, too—I mean, does he lose his temper easily?"

Lex glared at her. "I refuse to answer that question on the ground that it might incriminate me. Why, it's as bad as that old gag: Answer Yes or No—have you stopped beating your wife?"

Cherry giggled. "Well, have you?"

"You know perfectly well that I have no wife," Lex retorted. "Also that I do *not* lose my temper easily."

"All right," Cherry said placatingly, "we'll leave you out of it. Does the mayor lose his temper easily?"

"Why do you ask?" Lex demanded suspiciously. "I told you that he's famous for his good disposition."

"No, you didn't," Cherry corrected him. "And more than once you mentioned the possibility of a political murder. Who's going to murder whom?"

Lex heaved his shoulders exasperatedly. "Cy wouldn't hurt a fly, but his supporters could make things so unpleasant for Harry Jenner that he'd have to leave town and practice law somewhere else. That's what I meant by a political murder."

"H-m-m," said Cherry thoughtfully. "Doesn't that kind of thing work both ways? You did say that Harry is hot-tempered. Isn't there a possibility that he and his supporters could make things so unpleasant for the mayor that *he* would have to leave town?"

"Not a chance," Lex replied. "You must have been asleep on the drive up when I told you that. But I'm beginning to suspect that, although Cy may not be the Little People's Choice, he *is* the Big People's Choice."

Cherry hesitated. The clue to the mayor's sudden fit of anger must lie in that crumpled front page which she had impulsively tucked into her handbag. Why shouldn't she produce it now and tell Lex what she had seen in the mirror?

"Let's stop talking politics," Lex said grumpily. "You haven't met Harry Jenner yet and you're talking as though you were going to go all out for him. If you're going to poke your pretty finger into the political pie, let me remind you again that you're not qualified to vote on Election Day."

Cherry smiled inwardly, thinking, "Lex hasn't changed a bit since he was a moody intern forever getting jealous without cause." Aloud she said, "Speaking of pie, let's have it for dessert—à la mode."

Lex immediately brightened. "Pumpkin or apple?"

"On second thought," Cherry said cheerfully, "all of your talk about Revolutionary times has changed my appetite. I'll have the Martha Washington cream pie, please."

At that very moment someone came in from the street and as though by magic Lex recovered completely from his sulks. "It's Dr. Clem," he whispered to Cherry as he slid off his stool and strode toward the door.

Cherry unhooked her heels and whirled around. A large and truly Teddy-bearish sort of man was hanging his battered brown felt hat on the rack. His graying brown hair was rumpled, and his gray-brown tweed suit looked as though it had never been pressed.

He lumbered rather than walked and clumsily slapped Lex on the shoulder. "Hiya, doc?"

"Just fine, sir, and you?" Lex replied with such humility that again Cherry almost fell off her stool.

What she did do was slide immediately to her feet to show her own personal respect for the doctor who had just come into the diner. Since neither one of them was in "whites" she didn't have to do this, but there was something about Dr. Clem which made her want to do it. But Lex's broad shoulders were in the way, and without even a nod to Cherry, Dr. Clem moved to the counter and said:

"The same as usual, Ben."

Ben immediately produced a piece of cheesecake and drew a cup of coffee from the huge urn. "Hot for this time of the year, isn't it, doc?"

"Well, no," Dr. Clem replied. "Unseasonably warm." Then, as he apparently caught Cherry's reflection in the mirror, he turned to Lex and said, "Why are you trying to hide that pretty lady from me?"

Lex gulped and moved slightly. "I wasn't—I mean, I was just about to introduce you."

Dr. Clem chuckled. "I already know who she is. Those cheeks are a dead giveaway. Good evening, Cherry. Hot for this time of the year, isn't it?"

Cherry grinned. "Why, no, Dr. Brown. Unseasonably warm, but—"

His broad shoulders shook with laughter as he reached around Lex to take her hand. "I'm Dr. Clem," he said. "Let's get that straight. I don't like to get confused with Dr. Brown who's a young medico around here, barely out of swaddling clothes, like Lex. Nice youngsters, both of 'em, but what they don't know would fill a medical library. How much do you know, Cherry?" he asked suddenly.

"I—I—" Cherry stammered, "I guess what I don't know would fill two medical libraries."

He nodded approvingly and hitched himself onto the stool. "Nobody in the medical profession really knows anything. That's why we're called practitioners. We practice on our patients and we seldom practice what we preach. For instance, we're forever telling our patients to get lots of rest and sleep, but how much rest and sleep do we get ourselves?"

Cherry knew it was a rhetorical question, so she simply seated herself and smiled.

"Now take this cheesecake and coffee," Dr. Clem continued between mouthfuls, "nothing could be worse for me at this hour of the night. Why didn't I order a bowl of warm gruel?"

Cherry and Lex ate their dessert in silence as the older doctor went on:

"The point is that I'm not convinced that gruel would be better for me than cheesecake and coffee. So, since I don't like gruel . . ." He left the sentence unfinished and shook his head. "Doctors and nurses are notoriously the worst patients in the world. It's because we have so little patience with theories. Every scientific fact is based on a theory. I, personally, have never been convinced that one and one make two. Can you think of any reason, Cherry, why they shouldn't make three or four?"

Cherry thought hard, frantically trying to remember the algebra and geometry she had learned in high school.

"Furthermore," Dr. Clem informed her gravely, "no two human beings are exactly alike. That *is* a proven fact. Don't you ever forget it while you're working for me."

"No, sir," Cherry said meekly. "I mean, yes, sir, I won't forget."

He set down his empty coffee cup. "Good. That's all you need to know. Now, I know all of your good points, but what I'm interested in are your weaknesses. What are they, Cherry, outside of being young and pretty?"

Cherry took a deep breath. "Well, when I was in training I was known as the late Miss Ames because sometimes I was almost late to classes. And I'm apt to let my imagination and curiosity run away with me. And when somebody makes me really good and mad I lose my temper—"

"But never with patients," Lex put in loyally. "Cherry is always very patient with really sick people."

Dr. Clem nodded. "Good. Good. When Lola Wright first came to work for me, Cherry, she was as young and pretty as you are. She was sometimes almost late, and she sometimes lost her temper. She hasn't changed much in the last twenty years, and neither have I. Wouldn't want a nurse who was a lot different from Lola. And I may as well confess that I'm partial to brunettes. Can you start to work tomorrow?"

"Oh, yes!" Cherry gasped. This was the most unorthodox interview of her whole career!

"Be as late as you like," he said. "Only time I'm fussy is when I have a patient coming in before his breakfast for a basal metabolism test. Otherwise, I won't expect you until around nine. Morning office hours are from ten to noon. Evening office hours from six to eight, except for Thursdays and Saturdays. No office hours on Sunday. You'll have plenty of free time on other days, but the hours will have to be flexible. Will you mind not being able to make plans until the last minute?"

"Not at all," Cherry told him. "I don't know a soul around here except Lex, so I probably won't make any dates."

Dr. Clem chuckled. "Except with Lex? Don't worry, Cherry, you'll meet some nice folks real soon. You'll like my patients and they'll like you. You mustn't get stuck on me the way Lola is. She's turned down about twenty good proposals of marriage just because she thought I couldn't get along without her. Now that was just plain silly of her, wasn't it?"

"Yes, sir—I mean, no, sir," Cherry said bewilderedly.

"Lola's a fine woman," Dr. Clem went on, "but stubborn as a mule. Kept telling her she could get married and have children and keep on working for me in her spare time. But she wouldn't listen, so I had to fire her."

"Y-you fired her?" Cherry stammered. "I thought she resigned."

"That's what *she* thinks," Dr. Clem retorted, grinning broadly. "I used a bit of psychology, that's all. Hinted that she was old enough to retire. She swallowed the bait, hook, line, and sinker—and quit. Old at forty? Why, she's in the prime of life! Lew Barker, who owns the drugstore next door, has been waiting for her ever since she went into training." He rubbed his hands together gleefully. "After their honeymoon in Florida she'll come back to work for me just as though she'd gone off on a vacation. Won't miss her a bit. I can tell already that you'll be just as good a hostess and housekeeper as she is. See you in the morning." He lumbered out through the door into the street.

"He could use two nurses, and that's a fact," Ben said with a sigh. "Forgot his hat as usual, but he'll be around in the morning to pick it up."

"He forgot to pay you, too," Lex said with a chuckle.

Ben shook his head. "He has a charge account with me, and I'd like to make the same arrangement with Miss Cherry, if she'd find it convenient. I guess you'll be staying with Miss Marcia," he said to Cherry, "and she doesn't serve meals. I sure would appreciate your patronage, especially so if, whenever you come in, you'd find time to pay a visit to Maria."

A few minutes later when Lex helped Cherry into the front seat of his car he explained:

"Ben's wife is a polio victim. They live in a tiny apartment above the back of the coffee shop. Dr. Clem visits

Maria almost every day. When he can't, Lola does—not to give her medication, because there isn't anything in the field of medicine which can put life into her legs. She was terribly depressed when she first learned that she would never walk again. Dr. Clem kept her alive with large doses of his practical psychology. He'll expect you to keep up the good work, so try to eat there as often as you can. While waiting for Ben to fill your order you can run up and have a little chat with Maria."

"I will," Cherry solemnly promised.

Lex turned on the ignition and started the motor. "Dr. Clem was right; no two persons are alike. Maria in her wheel chair is one of the most cheerful persons you'll ever meet. But Miss Marcia, who has loads of friends and only a slight limp to handicap her, is as sour as curdled cream. It doesn't make sense. That accident —whatever it was—couldn't have changed her personality so drastically. I've often wondered what did happen to make her so grim."

"Is she really very bitter, Lex?" Cherry asked.

"Yes," he said quietly, "she is. I don't want you to feel unhappy about living at The Manor, because, after all, you won't see much of Miss Marcia. But I think you ought to know, so that you can be prepared for the worst. Sometimes Miss Marcia acts as though she had no heart at all!"

~~~~~~~~~~~~~~~~~~~~~~~~~~~~~~~~~~~~~~

CHAPTER V

The Manor

THEY DROVE ALONG MAIN STREET AND CHERRY CAUGHT glimpses on both sides of neat churches, large and small stores, a school, and a library. Lex stopped at a red light and pulled over to the curb.

"Ahead of us," he said, "is the avenue which divides the old part of town from the new residential section. And on our left, occupying the whole corner—behold! —The Manor."

Cherry leaned across the steering wheel to peer at the big sprawling house. "Why, in this light," she said, "it looks like three houses."

"Exactly," Lex replied. "The middle section of it is stone and it was originally a sort of castle-fortress, as most of the Dutch manor houses were in the seventeenth century. The two wooden wings, the porches, the peaked roof, and the dormer windows were added by later generations, in the eighteenth and nineteenth

53

centuries. So now there are twenty rooms and each one is a historical gem."

"My goodness," Cherry gasped, half-laughing, half-serious. "I'm not too sure that I want to live in a museum."

"Cheer up," Lex said consolingly. "It won't look so gloomy in bright daylight. And the real museum is the little old Dutch part of the house which you'll probably never be permitted to see. It's about the size of a large duplex apartment and that's where Miss Marcia lives. The two old family servants occupy rooms above the huge East Parlor where Miss Marcia is undoubtedly waiting to receive you with regal formality. I wish she would receive you in her sanctum sanctorum because I've never seen it. Only Miss Marcia's cronies are permitted to cross that threshold, but according to the pictures which the *Sun* publishes every now and then in its Know Your Hudson column, Miss Marcia does indeed live in a priceless museum."

"Twenty rooms," Cherry repeated wonderingly. "It's really more of an inn than a boardinghouse."

Lex nodded. "A lot of people have tried to buy The Manor from Miss Marcia, so they could convert it into an inn, but she won't part with it or any part of it. I understand that even when she was desperate for money she turned down a fabulous offer for the tiles in her fireplace which were imported by her ancestors from Delft, Holland." He came around to Cherry's side of the car and helped her climb out to the sidewalk. Then he took her bag from the back. "I guess you can under-

stand now what I meant when I said that Miss Marcia
is a real old-timer."

"But why does she take in boarders?" Cherry asked.
"Her ancestors must have been very rich—"

"Lords of the manor in all senses of the phrase," Lex
said as they waited on the corner for the light to turn
green. "Her parents were well off, too, I understand. I
don't know how they lost their money—if they did. All
I know is that Miss Marcia was educated at the best
schools here and abroad, and was the belle of the town
when she was your age. But when she emerged from
mourning shortly after the death of her parents about
a quarter of a century ago, she began to take in boarders. Many of her guests, as she calls them, who took
rooms and suites then are still there. And the servants
date back to Miss Marcia's youth, too. Coombs, the
major-domo, was the old family butler, and Mrs. Briggs,
the housekeeper, was Mrs. Charlton's personal maid.
They are both very prim and proper, so watch your step,
Miss Ames."

They crossed the street and Cherry said, "I'll be the
soul of dignity. I promise not to let my curiosity run
away with me, but it all seems terribly baffling now."

They climbed the wide steps to the porch and Lex
lifted the brass knocker on the front door. Almost simultaneously the door was opened by an elderly man who
Cherry knew must be the major-domo.

"Good evening, Dr. Upham." He bowed slightly,
took Cherry's bag, and bowed in her direction. "Miss
Ames, I presume."

Cherry suppressed a giggle, thinking, "If he had sideburns, I'd be carried back to the Victorian era." Aloud she said primly, "Good evening, Coombs."

He stepped backward into the hall and with a barely perceptible motion of his eyelids indicated that they should follow him. Cherry was grateful for the reassuring touch of Lex's hand on her elbow as they moved down the narrow passageway. Then she forgot herself completely when they crossed the threshold of one of the most beautiful rooms she had ever seen.

"It's a real withdrawing room," she thought, admiring the walnut-toned mahogany chest of drawers above which hung an Adam carved-and-gilt mirror. Heavy draperies were drawn across the long windows but several table lamps shed a pleasing glow on the faded blue wall-to-wall carpet. In the cupboard part of a Sheraton secretary were rare pieces of Staffordshire pottery and delicate enamels. Attractively grouped in various corners of the huge room were Chippendale chairs and Hepplewhite tables.

"Miss Ames and Dr. Upham," the butler intoned. At the same moment Cherry saw that a lady was seated in one of the Georgian armchairs. She was so motionless and her face so expressionless that Cherry felt sure she must be a wax doll. But when the butler bowed himself out of the room, she stood up. She was wearing a long-sleeved black moiré gown with a long, full skirt that rustled faintly as she moved slowly toward Cherry and extended a small, thin hand.

It was the gesture of royalty and Cherry was seized

Miss Marcia's face was so expressionless that she looked like a wax doll

with the desire to drop a curtsy. Lex said with formal dignity:

"Miss Marcia, may I present Miss Cherry Ames?"

Miss Marcia's lips barely moved. "How do you do?" Cold finger tips touched Cherry's hand. "A pleasure, I'm sure." Cherry heard herself babble: "It is very kind of you to let me stay here."

"Since you are here," was Miss Marcia's cold reply, "I assume that Dr. Clemuel Brown has decided to engage your services." She dismissed Lex with a queenly gesture of her head. "We will not detain you from your duties at the hospital any longer, Dr. Upham. Thank you. Good night."

Lex gave Cherry a surreptitious wink and departed. When Cherry heard the front door close, a momentary sense of panic swept over her. It was all so unreal that she felt as though she had been touring a museum with a class from school and had been left behind at closing time. She clenched her fists, fighting an overwhelming urge to turn and run after Lex. Then she said:

"I hope my arriving so late in the evening hasn't inconvenienced you, Miss Charlton."

"Quite all right," the regal landlady said, "but unfortunately my housekeeper, Mrs. Briggs, has already retired for the night, so I shall have to show you to your room." She led the way down the hall and started up the stairs, moving with such grace, in spite of her handicap, that Cherry was amazed. Her lameness was only betrayed by the fact that she stopped for a fleeting second on each step and gripped the banister firmly before taking the next one.

The broad staircase ended in another long carpeted hall off which were many closed doors. But the one closest to the stairs was ajar, and as Miss Marcia reached inside to press a wall button, the room was flooded with light.

"Oh, it's beautiful!" Cherry exclaimed.

"It is quite small," Miss Marcia said tonelessly, "but I trust it will be satisfactory. It is one of the few single rooms which has a private bath."

The room *was* small but the furniture seemed just right: a sleigh bed, a cylinder-front writing desk, a ladder-back armchair, and a comfortable-looking chaise longue which was obviously *not* a period piece since Cherry's suitcase was reposing on it.

"That's where I'll do my own reposing when I'm not in bed," Cherry quickly decided. "Lacking a quilled pen, I can't see myself writing a letter at that antique desk, and I'd have to lose a lot of weight before I'd dare sit in that chair with its bamboo legs."

Her landlady's cold voice interrupted her thoughts. "These are our rules and before you retire for the night I must insist that you understand them thoroughly and assure me that you will follow them to the letter." She pointed to a framed sampler on the wall above the lowboy which Cherry hadn't noticed before. In the exact center of the sampler was a typewritten list which looked so incongruously out of place that Cherry blinked unbelievingly. Laughter bubbled up inside her as she read:

KEYS: None are permitted. This includes keys to the front and back doors of the establishment.

CLOSING TIME: 11 P.M. Any guest who remains out on the streets after that hour will have to remain on the streets.

MEALS: None are served and none may be prepared in the rooms. This includes boiling water for tea or eggs.

LIGHTS: With the exception of those in the halls and public baths, all must be extinguished before midnight.

MAIL: This is placed in the individual rooms twice daily by Coombs. The establishment is not responsible for outgoing mail.

LAUNDRY: None whatsoever is permitted in the rooms. This includes the use of an electric iron. Guests requiring laundry and pressing service should contact Mrs. Briggs.

PETS: None are permitted. This includes parrots, canaries, cats, toy dogs, squirrels, and white mice.

ENTERTAINING: None whatsoever is permitted. This includes the possession of radios, television sets, and record players.

VISITORS: Admitted between the hours of 5–7 P.M. For this purpose the East Parlor is available for guests occupying the East Wing; the West Parlor for guests occupying the West Wing.

Cherry's eyes were caught first by the rules concerning laundry and pressing. Thank goodness the borrowed uniforms in her suitcase were nylon, so the wrinkles would probably shake out overnight! Then she read the rules concerning pets and she had to bite her lips to keep from laughing.

But Miss Marcia was staring at her as suspiciously as though she were positive Cherry had secreted a white rabbit in her suitcase. "Do you quite understand the rules?" she asked frigidly.

"Oh, yes," Cherry replied, sobering immediately. "But I can't help wondering about some of your rules . . . the one concerning meals, for instance. Surely that one isn't rigid. Do your elderly guests have to go out for their meals—even in a blizzard?"

Miss Marcia's black eyes flashed as she drew herself up to her full height, and Cherry realized that her landlady was anything but a wax doll. She was as tall and alive as Cherry was herself. In the bright lights from the ceiling bulbs Cherry could see that Miss Marcia had jet-black hair which was only white at the temples, and though she wore it severely pulled back from her slender face into a braided figure eight, Cherry could tell from the tendrils above her ears and at the nape of her neck that Miss Marcia had naturally curly hair.

"She must have been a truly beautiful woman once," Cherry thought, "and she could be even more beautiful now if only the expression on her face were not so stern and forbidding."

"The rules," Miss Marcia was declaiming, "are rigid

in every respect. Let that be strictly understood here and now."

"I'm sorry," Cherry said apologetically. "I only asked because, as a nurse—well, I think about those things. I know that if someone were ill you'd let me fix him or her a cup of tea."

Miss Marcia folded her arms. "I certainly would not! If anyone in this establishment becomes indisposed, he or she is taken at once to the hospital or to the nursing home, depending upon the decision of the attending physician. Above all else, I want you to understand that you are here as my guest, not in any professional capacity."

Cherry's red cheeks flamed, as much from anger as from embarrassment. Such a hard, fast rule concerning illnesses seemed to her to be based on cold-blooded cruelty. At that moment she disliked her landlady so much that she wanted to leave the "establishment" at once.

"Furthermore," Miss Marcia continued, "it must be strictly understood here and now that should you yourself become ill, you may send for any doctor in the vicinity with the exception of Dr. Clemuel Brown. No matter what happens, he is not permitted to cross the threshold of my home." With the flick of one slim finger she switched off the bright overhead lights, leaving the room in darkness except for the faint glow from small lamps on the matching consoles which flanked the sleigh bed.

Cherry heard the rustle of skirts as her landlady

added crisply, "This is, however, a free country. My maternal ancestors fought for our independence. If you do not wish to abide by my rules, you may depart in the morning and I shall not charge you a penny for your overnight stay." The door was closed quietly but with an emphatic click.

Cherry's anger immediately gave way to the laughter which she had kept bottled up for so long. Giggling silently as she unpacked her uniforms, she asked herself:

"Did you ever meet anyone quite so inconsistent as Miss Marcia Charlton? Wouldn't let you stay here until after Dr. Clem had approved of you, but now states that he must never be permitted to enter these sacred portals! I'll bet she's just as inconsistent about her house rules."

The closet was tiny but the bathroom which adjoined it was even tinier. Cherry took a shower, resisted the temptation to wash her stockings and undies, donned pajamas, and climbed into bed. The ticking of the alarm clock, which she had borrowed from Gwen, reminded her that she must set it for seven, and while doing so, she remembered the rule about lights. But switching off the lamps on the console tables left her in utter darkness. That, in such a strange house, was more than Cherry could bear. Hastily she groped her way to the windows and yanked at the drawstrings which pulled aside the heavy chintz draperies. Light from the broad avenue streamed into the room. Cherry defiantly opened a window, thinking, "There's probably some rule about the evils of night air, but I don't care," and climbed wearily into bed.

And then she heard sounds which made her sit bolt upright. Someone in the room below, which must be that fabulous East Parlor, was weeping. The sobs were so muffled that if she hadn't opened her window she wouldn't have heard them. A truck rumbled by and then there was silence.

Cherry sank back on the pillow. Who could be crying at this time of night when surely everyone else in the whole huge house must be sound asleep? Could it be her landlady? What was it Lex had said about Miss Marcia?

"Rumor hath that she was once as young and gay and beautiful as you—"

"Another time, it seemed to me that she was trying so hard not to cry that—"

Cherry fell asleep, asking herself a lot of questions which she felt sure she could never answer. One of them was:

What could possibly have happened in Miss Marcia's youth to change her so drastically?

CHAPTER VI

First Day on Duty

CHERRY AWOKE THE NEXT MORNING A FULL MINUTE before the alarm clock was due to go off. At first she didn't know where she was and stared around the room at the priceless antiques in amazement. Then the door from the hall opened and a middle-aged woman bustled in. She was wearing a green uniform and a large white apron. Her yellowish-gray hair was piled on top of her head in a bygone fashion and held in place by a large velvet bow. The white collar and cuffs of her green uniform were stiffly starched, and folded across her arms were snowy towels.

"Good morning, Miss Ames," she said crisply, "I'm Briggs."

At that moment, to Cherry's embarrassment, the alarm went off. Hastily she silenced it and slid out of bed. "Good morning, Mrs. Briggs. If I'd known you were going to wake me up, I wouldn't—"

"Never mind, never mind." The housekeeper bustled

into the bathroom and bustled out again, her arms free. "It won't happen again. I would have brought you fresh towels last night if I'd known for sure that you were going to occupy this room." She closed the window with a disapproving bang. Arms akimbo now, she surveyed Cherry critically. "So you're going to take Miss Lola's place?"

"I'm going to try to," Cherry said humbly.

Mrs. Briggs shrugged. "It's a large order, and I tell you what. I feel so sorry for you, new to town and trying to step into Miss Lola's shoes, that I'll fix you a bite of breakfast this first morning if you'll dress real quickly and come down to the kitchen by the back stairs at the far end of the hall."

She bustled off, leaving Cherry with mixed feelings. Mrs. Briggs was not, apparently, as cold-blooded as her mistress, but stepping into Lola Wright's shoes was not going to be easy. Half an hour later Cherry timidly entered an unbelievably large kitchen and immediately wished that she hadn't. Coombs, departing at that moment through the swinging door to the butler's pantry, gave her such a disapproving look that Cherry knew he would report her violation of the rules concerning meals to his mistress promptly.

But Mrs. Briggs said cheerfully, "Pay no attention to himself. Pull up a chair and sit down. Here, I kept the griddle cakes warm for you, and there's plenty of hot coffee." She seated herself opposite Cherry and continued, "This can never happen again, of course, but I felt I ought to tell you. Miss Lola is a very lovely person and a very lovable person. You're much prettier than she ever was, and maybe everyone will learn to love you. But right off they won't." She shook her head dolefully. "Not one of Dr. Clem's patients is going to like this change. Not one of them."

Cherry's appetite fled but she forced herself to eat. Mrs. Briggs was certainly an enigma; she seemed to be warm and friendly and cheerful but everything she said was so depressing. Cherry stood up. "I don't think I care for any coffee, thank you, Mrs. Briggs. I'd better be running along."

"Run!" The housekeeper sniffed. "Nobody could run for ten long blocks. And it's only eight o'clock. Miss Lola won't be there until three minutes after nine. She always stops off at the post office first to pick up the mail, you know."

Cherry didn't know and she sank helplessly back in the kitchen chair, wondering if she ever would know all the rules and regulations which seemed to be important factors in her new job.

"Sit down," Mrs. Briggs said in a commanding tone of voice. "A nice cup of hot coffee will perk you up and prepare you for what's coming. I feel that it's my duty to start you off right."

Cherry suddenly made up her mind. Mrs. Briggs wasn't really warm and friendly at all. She was doing her best to start Cherry off on the *wrong* foot. She, like Coombs, probably would report this violation of the rules concerning meals to Miss Marcia and make it sound as though Cherry had insisted upon having breakfast at The Manor. It was high time that Cherry Ames, R.N., stood up for her rights and made a few rules of her own.

She started out by standing up again and saying quietly, "No coffee, thank you, Mrs. Briggs. And after this it will not be necessary for you to wake me up in the morning. I have an alarm clock, remember? Now, about my laundry. I should like to make arrangements to have it done here on the premises if it is not too expensive. However, since my uniforms are an important item, I shall consult Miss Lola Wright about that before making a decision." With her head held high, Cherry marched out to the long, narrow hall. She felt sure that she had made an enemy of Mrs. Briggs, but she felt equally sure that Mrs. Briggs had never been a friend and never really would be one.

Cherry's one hope now was that Lola Wright would prove to be a friend. The question was, Should she appear in uniform or carry along her whites? Normally she would never have thought of walking ten blocks in uniform, but in this small town the rules probably were different. Perhaps Lola would expect her to appear ready for duty. . . .

By the time Cherry had climbed the steep back stairs, she had decided to stick to the regular rules of her profession. When she emerged in the upstairs hall, the long row of closed doors was confusing. She knew that her room was close to the top of the front stairs but she hesitated between two doors. Finally she opened one of them and discovered that it was a closet. Hastily she closed it and tried the other one which did open into her room.

Hardly had she crossed the threshold when Mrs. Briggs appeared as mysteriously as though she had dropped from the sky. "Well, Miss Snoopy," the housekeeper said accusingly, "what, may I ask, were you doing in that closet?"

"I wasn't in it," Cherry pointed out impatiently. "And it seems to me that you're the snoopy one. The very idea of your tiptoeing down the hall, so you could spy on me!"

"I did not tiptoe," Mrs. Briggs said angrily. "I'll have you know that I am very light on my feet and these halls are thickly carpeted."

"All right," Cherry said, regaining her temper. "I apologize for opening the wrong door by mistake. But you must realize that this is my first morning here and all of the doors look exactly alike to me."

The housekeeper sniffed. "We've heard that you fancy yourself as a detective. Well, if you know what's good for you, you'll mind your own business." She stepped backward into the hall and closed the door with a sharp click.

Cherry shrugged. Mai Lee had thoughtfully provided her with a collapsible overnight bag and in it Cherry now packed a uniform, white stockings, white shoes, and a Spencer cap. She had brought with her from home her own Spencer pin and the bandage scissors which she never traveled without. Winning those scissors had been one of the very first exciting steps in her career.

She glanced at her wrist watch, which Charlie had given her when she left Hilton to go into training, and saw that it was not quite eight thirty. It was too early to leave for Dr. Clem's office, but Cherry decided to start off, so she could walk slowly and do a bit of sightseeing, and also because she felt so unhappy in this beautiful but gloomy house.

Out on the street she took a deep breath of the cold, crisp air and felt better. The sidewalk was jammed with children hurrying to school, and as she mingled with them, her spirits rose. Everything was going to be all right, in spite of Mrs. Briggs' prediction that nobody would like her at first. The housekeeper was a trouble-making busybody and Miss Marcia Charlton was a sour old maid, but Cherry didn't expect to see much of them, so she dismissed them from her mind and looked forward to the pleasure of meeting Miss Lola Wright.

The clock in the Town Hall tower was striking the hour when Cherry turned into Dr. Clem's neat brick walk. Standing on the stoop was a tall, thin woman who was wearing a nurse's cape over her uniform. When she heard Cherry's footsteps she turned and with a wide smile called out:

"Hi, Cherry Ames. I'm Lola Wright. My, but you're punctual!"

Cherry hurried forward to shake hands, then Lola unlocked the door and led the way into the vestibule.

"This is where the patients leave their coats, rubbers, galoshes, and such," she said, opening another door which brought them into the waiting room. Lola hurried across it to the desk at the far end, dumped the mail she had been carrying, and without even shedding her cape picked up the phone, pressed a button, and dialed a number.

"The Telephone Answering Service," she said over her shoulder to Cherry. "I always call them right off the bat to let them know I'm here and to take any messages which may have come in since Dr. Clem left at eight." She began to scribble on a pad, frowning with concentration and muttering little "ums."

Cherry took off her red flannel coat and glanced around the attractive but cheerfully informal waiting room. Sunlight was streaming through the clean picture windows which faced east. The sofas and chairs were invitingly comfortable-looking and here and there were well-kept potted plants, vases of giant bronze chrysanthemums, magazine racks, modern floor lamps, and conveniently placed end tables. Cherry noticed with satisfaction that the bottom shelf of one long table was filled with children's books and puzzles. The walls were painted a soothing shade of blue and were decorated with a few bright-colored Hudson River Valley landscapes. Most of them were water colors and had been affectionately inscribed to Dr. Clem by the artists, obviously gifts from patients, but from men and women who were by no means amateurs.

"Well, that's that!" Lola Wright's crisp, cheery voice

broke into Cherry's thoughts. "Come on! Here's our little dressing room. Leave your coat here where I leave my cape and get into uniform." She patted her cap into place and said, "I wear my whites to work because I live across the street, you know. In the apartment above the drugstore. I started out with Miss Marcia, but frankly I couldn't stand it. When Mrs. Barker offered me her spare room, I snapped it up. How do you like living at The Manor?"

"Not very much, so far," Cherry said as she changed into uniform. "But I haven't been there long enough to judge. I met Mrs. Briggs this morning and she's certainly a great admirer of yours."

"Briggs!" Lola Wright snorted. "I could have endured that prissy Miss Marcia, but Briggs and Coombs —well, I just couldn't endure their snoopy, snooty attitudes." Suddenly she collapsed on the narrow bench in the dressing room and gave way to gales of laughter. "Oh, Cherry dear, how foolish I am. I left The Manor at about the same time you were born. Here I am rambling along as though we were the same age when actually I'm old enough to be your mother."

"You don't look it," Cherry said truthfully as she donned her perky cap. Lola Wright was tall and too thin for her height, and her jet-black hair was streaked with gray, but there was nothing old-maidish about *her*. She moved and talked and laughed with the spontaneity of youth. "And I'll never be as efficient as you are," Cherry added. "Suppose I forget to call the Answering Service the minute I come in?"

"You won't," Lola assured her as they went back to her desk in the waiting room. "The phone itself would remind you. Answering Service doesn't take the call, you see, unless it rings three times and nobody here answers it. But when they know I'm here they may let it ring four or even five times, because they know that often I can't answer it right away. But let's start at the beginning. First you pick up the mail. If you walked from The Manor, you passed the post office which is right next to the Cameo across the street." Cherry nodded. "Now's here's the batch I picked up this morning. All of these, as you can see, are ads from pharmaceutical firms. I clip them all together and put them in this folder for Dr. Clem to read when he has time. Some of the booklets contain valuable information; others are worthless, but he is the only one who can decide the difference. He is especially interested in new drugs which are stocked in the hospital pharmacy and never prescribes anything which hasn't received its stamp of approval."

Cherry chuckled. "From the way he talked to me last night I might have thought that all of his patients were human guinea pigs."

"Exactly the opposite is true," Lola said. "He views with suspicion anything but good old-fashioned aspirin, but somehow manages to keep himself amazingly well informed on all the latest medical wrinkles. Now these envelopes, as you can see, are obviously from patients and probably contain checks. That's why I pick up the mail instead of having it delivered." She began to slit open the envelopes with a pretty handmade brass paper knife which Cherry guessed was another gift from a patient. "Never, *never* let Dr. Clem get hold of payments which are made by mail. Not until you have recorded said payments in the ledger. He is very careless about checks. He has been known to write out directions to patients on the back of them, also memos to himself which he promptly loses. The only safe way is first record the payments in the ledger; then get Dr. Clem to endorse the checks. Once or twice a week I make deposits in the bank, which, by the way, is right next door to the post office. The duplicate deposit slip I bring back to Dr. Clem, but I don't let him have it until I've seen him with my own eyes make the entry in his checkbook." She shook her head sorrowfully. "Things would be much simpler around here if he'd let me keep his checkbook for him. No, I don't really mean that, since he pays most of his bills according to a barter system which is beyond me."

Cherry moaned. "Frankly, the whole bookkeeping part of this job terrifies me. Can you explain some of it to me right now?"

"Your part of it is simple," Lola said. "But let's stick to the routine. Switching on the sterilizer is one of your first *musts*, because Dr. Clem might come in before ten and treat an early patient." She led the way into the big treatment room which adjoined the doctor's consultation room. She switched on the sterilizer and pointed to the red light which immediately went on. "That'll remind you to turn it off after ten minutes or so. This lever, when you push it down, automatically turns off the current, opens the top, and raises the tray so that the instruments can drain."

Cherry followed Lola into another room which contained the X-ray and fluoroscope. "All you have to do in here," Lola said, "is dust. And that's next on the program. I've timed it so that I can do it all during the ten minutes that the sterilizer is on. Unless, of course, the phone rings constantly, which it sometimes does. Then the dusting just has to wait until after office hours." Another door from the X-ray room opened into a narrow passage which ended at the entrance to the laboratory. "On your right," said Lola, "is the darkroom and on your left is my housekeeping closet." In it were dustcloths, a dry mop, and a watering can with a long, thin spout. "For my plants and flowers," Lola explained as they began to work. "We have vitamins for them, too, on the very same shelf in the lab where free samples of vitamins for patients are kept. I clean the leaves on some of the plants with cotton soaked in castor oil. Makes 'em look so nice and shiny and healthy."

In the smaller treatment room, which also adjoined the consultation room, Cherry dusted the plastic cover on the electrocardiograph while Lola tidied the black leather couch. "In this closet," she told Cherry, "we keep the basal metabolism equipment, and on the shelf above it repose the rebozos."

"The what?" Cherry asked in dismay. "The word is

vaguely familiar, but I'm sure I didn't learn anything about rebozos when I was in training or working at the Hilton Clinic."

"I'll explain later." Lola dashed into the big treatment room to turn off the sterilizer and then into the consultation room to answer the phone. She moved so swiftly that Cherry, trotting after her, was out of breath when they met again at the housekeeping closet. "No more dirty work," Lola said. "We'll scrub at the sink in the lab and then I'll start you off on the bookkeeping. A lick and a promise is all this office ever needs because Mrs. Regan does the heavy cleaning on Thursday and Saturday afternoons when we don't have office hours. Her husband was killed in one of those inexplicable accidents which happen every now and then at night down by the railroad tracks. Dottie, who is eight years old, was born prematurely the next day, and Mrs. Regan was very ill for a long time afterward. Twelve-year-old Tommy is the oldest boy and his kid brother is nine. Their great-uncle, Tim O'Brien, lives with them in one of the town-owned tenements. The kids are forever coming in for treatment of minor cuts and bruises, so Mrs. Regan and Dr. Clem have one of those deals. She doesn't charge him for cleaning and he never sends her a bill."

"A very good arrangement," Cherry said approvingly. "But I'd better make a note of it; otherwise, I'd be sure to make a mistake and send Mrs. Regan a bill."

Lola shook her head. "If you started making notes of all the deals Dr. Clem has with his patients, you'd need a ledger bigger than this one." She opened the book on her desk. "But you won't make any mistakes because you always post from your day sheet to your accounts receivable in the ledger. Dr. Clem keeps the day sheet himself. Here's Saturday morning's day sheet. We'll post to the ledger from it right now, so you can see how easy it is."

Cherry stared at the sheet of ruled yellow paper which Lola had taken from the desk drawer. It was divided into five columns:

| | | SERVICE | | |
| HOUR | PATIENT | RENDERED | FEES | RECEIPTS |

"Take the first line across the sheet," said Lola:

| 8 A.M. | Mrs. Martha Deems | House Visit | $6.00 | $6.00 |

Mrs. Deems obviously paid in cash for the house call, but in order to avoid any possible confusion in the future, we'll post both amounts to her account in the ledger. Here's her page with her address and phone number. In the first blank column write the date. In the next: A.M. House Visit. Then, in both the debit and credit columns, the numeral six. Finally, on the day sheet, put a tiny penciled check mark by both numbers to show that the amounts have been posted to the ledger. Clear?"

"So far, yes," Cherry said dubiously. "Math was not my strong point in school, but I can see that although Mrs. Deems paid for the Saturday visit, she still owes eighteen dollars for two office visits and an X-ray."

"That's right," Lola said approvingly. "If this were the first of the month, you'd send her a statement for that amount. Now you sit down at the desk and see if you can handle the next transaction yourself."

"But it makes no sense," Cherry wailed. "Dr. Clem gave an antihistamine injection to somebody named Maria who paid him with a rebozo."

"Ved-dy simple," said Lola with a chuckle. She answered the phone, made a notation on the memo pad, and then went on, "Maria is married to Ben who owns the coffee shop on the opposite corner. Her legs are paralyzed but her hands are never idle. She is forever weaving on her hand loom lovely Spanish shawls— stoles, I guess you'd call them—the Mexican word is rebozo. Everyone in town buys them from her—they're featured at the Women's Exchange—because they make such lovely gifts. Around this time of the year Maria gets cold shots once a week and she pays Dr. Clem for them with a rebozo every time he calls. He treasures them and doles them out at Christmas to the feminine patients on his list. You know—gals he went to school with and such. Oh," she interrupted herself, "I guess I should have started out by saying that Maria lived in Mexico City until she married Ben and became an American citizen."

Cherry jumped, remembering now that Wade had promised to bring her a salmon-pink rebozo after his next flight to Mexico City. Now she knew what to expect.

"Last year," Lola went on, "Dr. Clem asked me to

give Maria her first injection and at the same time to pick out from her hanks of yarn the color which I thought would be most becoming to a brunette who had a few gray hairs. I chose a simply gorgeous salmon pink. I've forgotten the Spanish word for it, but it was one of the hanks Maria imported from Mexico—a typical Latin shade. I never saw anything quite like it. Anyway, I was thrilled because I naturally expected to receive that rebozo for Christmas, but I didn't. Instead, it mysteriously disappeared."

"What do you mean?" Cherry asked curiously.

"Well," said Lola, "when it was finished in December, Maria gave it to me and I put it on the shelf with the others. Then it vanished like magic. Nobody got it for Christmas. I know, because I wrap all of Dr. Clem's presents for him and deliver them myself. The only thing he does is write cute little messages on the cards and tell me what is for whom. No," she corrected herself, "that's not quite true. He does wrap my present, and is it ever a mess! You'd never believe that a man who so skillfully handles delicate instruments could be so clumsy with tissue paper and a bit of ribbon. Anyway, I was awfully disappointed when I got a lemon-colored rebozo for Christmas. What do you suppose happened to the salmon-pink one?"

"Could somebody have stolen it?" Cherry suggested. "It would be so easy for someone who was alone in the waiting room while you were in the darkroom."

Lola shook her head. "If it was stolen, Dr. Clem would have had a fit. I showed it to him before I put it in the closet and he vastly admired it; praised my good taste, made me model it for him, and all that sort of thing. So he couldn't have forgotten it, absent-minded as he sometimes is, when it came time to wrap them. When it wasn't with the others, then I took for granted that he'd taken it upstairs so that he could wrap it for me. But he didn't. Lex Upham says you're a famous amateur detective. What do you deduce, Madam Sherlock?"

Cherry grinned. "I strongly suspect that Dr. Clem is having a secret romance with a brunette who has a few gray hairs."

Lola snorted. "Dr. Clem is a dyed-in-the-wool bachelor. Oh, he's very fond of his lady patients, and especially Nellie Carson who simply adores him, but he has no secrets from me."

Cherry shrugged. "Is Nellie Carson a brunette with a few gray hairs?"

Lola snorted again. "She'd be snow-white if she didn't dye it. But goodhearted Nellie buys rebozos from Maria practically by the gross, so Dr. Clem wouldn't think of giving her one. Besides, she's so rich he usually sends her something funny from the ten-cent store with a cute card. Do me a favor, Cherry," she finished, "while I'm in Florida try to solve the mystery of the missing rebozo. I, too, suspect Dr. Clem, but I can't for the life of me provide him with a motive for stealing something from himself."

"It's all beyond me," Cherry admitted. "Not to change the subject, but before you go, will you give me your address in Florida so that I can send you a wire if I get into trouble?"

"You won't get into trouble, honey," Lola assured her. "And I won't have a permanent address. You see, I'm going with Lew Barker and his mother who has never been any farther from Sleepyside than New York City. So we'll be driving around visiting historic spots most of the time. Florida is simply our goal, but I imagine we'll spend several days in Washington and Gettysburg and places like that."

"Sounds like a honeymoon," Cherry said slyly.

Lola blushed, but before she could say anything, the front doorbell tinkled. Cherry glanced up and saw through the glass partition of the vestibule that the first patient had arrived. Almost simultaneously the phone rang and Dr. Clem came in from the side door that opened into the lab. The office hours had begun and Cherry felt completely incapable of coping with any part of the routine.

"Oh, why," she asked herself, "did I spend so much time chatting with Lola about a disappearing Mexican stole when the four-button phone system is still a baffling mystery to me?"

CHAPTER VII

Blue Monday

BUT AS THINGS TURNED OUT, CHERRY DISCOVERED THAT Lola had been right not to teach her too much of the routine all at once. For one thing, it was all so flexible and Dr. Clem was so eccentric that the word "routine" didn't really apply to any part of the morning office hours. Although Dr. Clem came in through the side door and could have gone straight to his consultation room without seeing or being seen by any of his patients, he lumbered through the lab and right into the waiting room to give the first patient a warm and friendly greeting. The elderly man whom Cherry had glimpsed through the glass partition was followed by several other patients, all of whom were welcomed by Dr. Clem as informally as though he were the host at a tea party. When they were all settled in the sofas and chairs to his satisfaction, he lumbered back to the desk for a consultation with Lola, who, in rapid-fire remarks, brought him up to date on the phone calls.

Their conversation sounded as though it were being carried on in a mysterious sort of shorthand to Cherry who hovered in the background:

"Mutter—Mrs. Um-m-m—mutter—the usual— m-m-m . . . Tell Mr. Mutter-m to come in this evening . . . I'll call on Mrs. Mumble-mumble after nursery school . . . mutter—mumble um-m-m—"

As they talked, Lola filled in prescription blanks which Dr. Clem signed, and then he suddenly turned around to greet Cherry as though she were his long-lost friend.

"Why, Cherry," he cried, "I didn't know you were here. I expected the late Miss Ames to be really late this first day. Especially after her first, ahem, night at The Manor. How are you, my dear? You look prettier in your uniform than I should have guessed. What is your favorite color? Red, I presume. You must pick out a rebozo for yourself shortly." He was still talking as he disappeared down the passageway into the X-ray room, and a moment later the buzzer announced that he was in the consultation room ready to receive the first patient.

As Lola ushered in the elderly man the phone rang. "Answer it, please, Cherry," she said over her shoulder.

Cherry picked up the phone, staring in alarm at the four buttons of the intercom system. "Dr. Brown's office. Miss Ames speaking."

"Oh," a voice said, "I must have the wrong number. I was calling Dr. Clem."

"This is Dr. Clem's office," Cherry said quickly.

"But you're not Lola," the woman said querulously.

"I'm the new nurse," Cherry explained. "Can I do anything for you?"

"We-ell," the woman said, "I'd rather speak to Lola."

Lola joined Cherry at the desk then and Cherry gratefully handed her the phone. As Lola talked to the patient, Cherry thought, "Mrs. Briggs' prediction is coming true already. Suppose none of the patients will have anything to do with me?"

Lola hung up and said in a low voice, "Don't look so glum, honey. As long as I'm around they're bound to prefer telling their troubles to me. So many of Dr. Clem's patients, like that woman, have known me since they were babies. Be firm with the next one. Simply say that I'm busy. Nine times out of ten all you'll have to do is switch the call to the extension in the consultation room."

"But I don't know how to do that," Cherry wailed. "I don't understand those buttons at all."

Lola smiled sympathetically. "When we first got the intercom system I was forever fouling up the buttons, but it's really easy once you get the idea. Let's take it in three easy steps. A patient calls and wants to talk to Dr. Clem. If he's in the consultation room, you simply buzz him by pressing the button labeled M.D. When Dr. Clem picks up the extension phone, you hang up this one. Clear?"

Cherry nodded.

"Sometimes," Lola continued, "a patient will call to ask a question which you can't answer without first consulting Dr. Clem. So you press the Hold button, then the Intercom button, and then you buzz him. When you and he have finished speaking, you reconnect yourself to the outside call by pressing the button labeled Our No. If you had forgotten to press the Hold button before switching to Intercom, you would have automatically been disconnected from the outside call."

Cherry moaned. "I'll never remember to press the Hold button, and the patient will be furious, especially if it's a long-distance call."

"We get very few of those," Lola said cheerfully. "And suppose you do accidentally disconnect an incoming call, so what? Just call the patient back. But to do that you must first push the button labeled Our No. which connects you with the Operator. Clear?"

"As mud," said Cherry gloomily.

"Practice makes perfect," Lola said. "So you sit right here and answer the phone from now on." She hurried off just as the phone rang. Cherry gingerly picked it up and said:

"Dr. Clem's office. Good morning."

"Oh, hello, Lola," a woman said cheerfully. "Have you got a cold or something? Your voice sounds different. But of course you never catch cold. What I called about was this: I don't want to bother Dr. Clem, but it suddenly dawned on me this morning when I was fixing breakfast that maybe Billy is due for his three-in-one booster shot. You know, whooping cough, diphtheria, and tetanus—or whatever you call it. Anyway, it seems to me, Lola, that he hasn't had one since he was six, and he's nine now, you know. Remember what a fuss he made? It was right after his birthday party. So silly of him. Look up his record, won't you, dear? His father could bring him over this evening, and maybe the baby too, because she's got sort of a sniffle. I'm sort of snuffly myself . . ." The young woman's voice ended in a sneeze and Cherry said hastily:

"Just a minute, please." Lola whisked by the desk at that moment on her way to the lab and Cherry grabbed the skirt of her uniform. "Now what do I do?" she whispered frantically. "Somebody wants to know about a triple toxoid booster shot. Where are the patients' card files kept?"

"In Dr. Clem's office," Lola said calmly. "You'd better buzz him right away because he's about to do a fluoroscopy."

The woman patient was still talking when Cherry said into the mouthpiece, "Who's calling, please?"

"Oh, Lola," the woman replied, "I guess I do have a cold if you didn't recognize my voice. It's Mabel. Do hurry. I'm frantically busy . . ."

"I'm sorry," Cherry interrupted, trying to make her voice sound both pleasant and firm at the same time, "but this is Dr. Clem's new nurse. If you'll give me your full name I'll look up Billy's—"

"Well, I never," the woman broke in impatiently. "Not Lola? Who are you and what are you doing in Dr. Clem's office? His new nurse? . . . Oh, I don't believe it. Is Lola really going to Florida? . . . I don't believe it. I simply can't. Well, anyway, I'm Mrs. Peck.

Mrs. William Peck. Please let me know about Billy Jr. right away. I'm so terribly busy . . ."

"Just hold on a minute, please." Cherry nervously pushed the Hold button, then the Intercom button, and buzzed the doctor.

"Hm," was his greeting.

"I'm sorry to bother you, Dr. Clem," Cherry said, "but Mrs. William Peck would like to know if—"

"Billy is due for his triple toxoid shot," he finished for her. "The answer is Yes and No." Click. He had hung up.

Lola was nowhere in sight and Cherry stared up at the ceiling for help. Suddenly she knew what the doctor had implied. She pushed the Our No. button and saw that the Intercom button promptly popped up. "Mrs. Peck? Billy *is* due for his shot, but since the polio season hasn't yet officially ended, Dr. Clem thinks it would be best to wait until perhaps the Thanksgiving holidays."

"Oh, yes!" Mrs. Peck exclaimed. "I do remember that Dr. Clem told me that last week when I brought little Jenny over for her checkup. Did you know that she's already tripled her birth weight? How could I have forgotten what he told me about Billy? It's because I'm so terribly busy. Well, good-by now."

Cherry put the phone back in the cradle but it rang again almost immediately. This patient, too, took it for granted that it was Lola who answered the phone and asked to speak to Dr. Clem. Cherry was about to switch the call when Lola appeared behind her.

"He's in the X-ray room," she said quietly. "See if you can't cope. If not, take the patient's phone number and we'll call her back later. It'll be some time, because I think that after the fluoroscopy Dr. Clem may want to take an X-ray."

"The doctor's busy right now," Cherry said into the mouthpiece. "This is Miss Ames, his new nurse. May I help you?"

"Oh!" the patient gasped. "Well, it's not very important. I'll call later or come in."

Several new patients arrived in the waiting room then and they all stared at Cherry as though she were a woman from Mars. When she introduced herself they smiled pleasantly and joined the general conversation. This, Cherry gathered in between phone calls, was mainly concerned with the coming election. Heated arguments ensued, and only one patient, an old man with a shock of curly white hair, remained aloof. He came in around eleven o'clock when one of the middle-aged women patients was declaiming loudly:

"I don't care what anybody says, our Mayor Cy is a lovely, generous person. Why, only yesterday he gave my little granddaughter a lollipop."

"Lollipops!" two men patients cried in unison. "Our children don't want candy. They want an education. Don't forget that Cy was against the new school. If you have any sense, Marge, you'll vote for Harry Jenner."

"Besides," a young woman added vehemently, "candy between meals is bad for our kids' teeth. Why doesn't our mayor know important things like that?"

Everyone began to talk at once—everyone except the bent old man who stood just inside by the vestibule door, huddled in his worn workman's jacket. His white hair was so long and shaggy that Cherry couldn't see much of his face, but she noticed that his patched jeans were very clean. He was so stoop-shouldered and frail-looking that she wished he would sit down somewhere in the crowded waiting room, but the only available space was the arm of a sofa. She started toward him, planning to offer him her chair behind the desk, when Lola beckoned her into the lab.

"Dr. Clem," she said hurriedly, "will cope with the patients and the phone calls from now on. He wants you to watch me do this urinalysis and then we'll develop those X-rays in the darkroom together. After that, I know he'll want me to do a blood count on Tim O'Brien, with you watching. Every doctor's lab technique is different, you know, so this will be your refresher course à la Dr. Clem."

Cherry glanced hastily around the laboratory and everything was so familiar that soon she felt right at home there: the Bunsen burner; the rack of graduated glass tubes which were called pipettes and were used for measuring small amounts of fluid; the various test tubes and graduates in assorted sizes—they all carried her back to the hours she had spent working in the labs at Spencer Hospital and Hilton Clinic. But she watched Lola carefully, listening attentively to every word, because this technique *was* slightly different; Dr. Clem used tablets instead of Benedict's solution in order to ascertain whether or not the specimen contained sugar.

"We had to use heat in my day," Lola said, lifting the glass cover from the microscope. "Here's where we keep the slides. Now you carry on, while I watch, not that it's necessary. You'll soon be giving Dr. Clem lessons."

When Cherry finished the urinalysis, Lola said, "Now for the darkroom, which is right next door. Do you think you need a refresher course in developing films?"

"I certainly do," Cherry said. "And since I can't very well watch you work in the pitch dark, couldn't we practice with a blank film?"

Lola frowned. "It's not exactly pitch dark in there. A tiny safety light in the ceiling goes on the minute you close the door. Also the exhaust fan, so you won't get asphyxiated. Once upon a time when I was working in an old-fashioned developing room the door got stuck and I—well, never mind. We can't practice now because Dr. Clem wants these pictures developed right away. If you don't mind sacrificing your time off this afternoon, we'll practice everything to your heart's content then."

"I'd love it," Cherry said. "But will you mind, Lola? After all, you're leaving early tomorrow."

"I'd love it too," Lola gaily. "It's fun working with you, Cherry. Now scram back to the waiting room and see if you can't make Tim O'Brien sit down until it's his turn to see the doctor. Tim was the last patient—the one with the mane of snow-white hair. Don't let him frighten you. He's only grouchy because he suffers

Frightfully from arthritis, but he won't come in for a treatment until he's paid Dr. Clem in advance. This he does by waxing the floors twice a month after his niece, Mrs. Regan, has given us a thorough cleaning."

"Another patient we never send a bill to?" Cherry asked weakly. "I'll never get the bookkeeping straight."

"Shoo," said Lola. "The bookkeeping is the least of your worries. Dr. Clem would be perfectly happy if you never sent out any bills. The only tough part of this job is that some mornings all of the young mothers come in with their infants, plus their two- and three-year olds. Then it's bedlam, equal only to some of the evenings when a lot of teen-age boys come in all at once. Usually they come in a gang after football, basketball, or base-ball games—minor casualties—and wow! That's how I got my gray hair. Now scram. Shoo. I have work to do."

Cherry went back to the waiting room and saw to her relief that Mr. Timothy O'Brien was seated on the edge of the sofa. He could have settled back comfortably against the cushions since he was the sole occupant, but he sat there stiffly, huddled in his jacket.

"It's awfully warm," Cherry said tentatively. "Could I help you take off your jacket, Mr. O'Brien?"

He acted as though he hadn't heard her, and Cherry, deciding to let well enough alone, retired behind the nurse's desk. But she felt as useless as the bowl of dwarf marigolds at her elbow. The attitude of the patients made this job hopelessly difficult. Obviously they weren't going to approve of anybody who tried to step into Lola Wright's shoes. And the office routine, although apparently simple, was so complicated by Dr. Clem's eccentricities that Cherry felt sure she could never learn the ropes in one short day. The chrysanthemums which were massed in the tall blue vase in the opposite corner of the room reminded her of her mother who probably was at this very moment exhibiting her prize specimens at the Hilton Garden Club Show. A wave of homesickness swept over Cherry. Just thinking about the cold beauty of The Manor made her regret more than ever that she was not now on a plane winging its way westward.

Then she squared her shoulders, scolding herself: "Don't be silly, Cherry Ames. The first day on duty at any job is always depressing. Remember how unpopular and inadequate you felt that first hectic evening when you started out as a night supervisor?"

That tour of duty had ended well, and so would this one!

~~~~~~

CHAPTER VIII

An Emergency

DR. CLEM USHERED OUT THE NEXT-TO-THE-LAST PA-
tient and said to the old man who was seated on the
edge of the sofa, "Come on in, Tim. How you been
doing? You're looking—" The closed door cut off the
rest of their conversation.

A time clock in the darkroom went off and Cherry
knew that meant the film had been in the developer for
three minutes. Lola would now dip the film in running
water ten times before putting it in the fixer where it
would remain for five minutes.

"I could have developed that X-ray," she scolded herself. "Why did I lose my nerve?"

The phone rang and a man said, "This is Mayor Hillman. Miss Ames?"

At last a patient who accepted the fact that Dr. Clem
had a new nurse! Gratefully Cherry said, "Yes, Mayor
Hillman. What can I do for you?"

"First," the mayor said considerately, "I'd like to

know how you're getting on at your new job? The first day is always difficult, but with such a good-natured boss and such an excellent teacher as Lola, I am sure you've had a very pleasant morning."

"Thank you, sir," Cherry said, thinking, "He *is* nice. Perhaps I exaggerated what I saw in the mirror last night."

"I was wondering," he continued affably, "if it would be convenient for me to drop in sometime this evening for a checkup. I'm feeling fine, just fine, but I feel sure I'm due for a routine physical. I'd like to drop in this evening around seven."

Cherry glanced swiftly at the appointment book. The page was blank, so she said, "I imagine that would be a good time, Mayor Hillman. We have no other definite appointments that I know of."

"Thank you, Miss Ames." He hung up. Cherry wrote his name down on the blank beside 7 P.M.

Lola came out of the darkroom and said, "The film's in running water now, where it'll stay for the next fifteen minutes. I never leave until this stage, do you?"

"No," Cherry agreed. "I seem to remember all of the steps now, but just let me go over them with you to be sure. First you put the blank film in the cassette, label it with the name of the patient, and lock it. Bring the cassette to the doctor in the X-ray room. After he has taken the picture, you bring the cassette back to the darkroom. Set the time clock at three. Turn out the light and close the door. Open cassette and take out film. Load it on the film-holder rack. Put it in the developer. Pull down lever on timer, so it will go off at the end of three minutes. Then—"

"That's enough," Lola interrupted. "You've obviously got it all down pat, so when the timer goes off again, you can pop in and put the film on the rack above the sink to dry." She glanced around the empty waiting room. "Um. Tim is in the consultation room now, huh? That means we'll be doing a blood count next. Maybe just a hemoglobin." She perched on the edge of the desk. "This has been an easy day, thank goodness. Not even one salesman to interrupt the routine. Although I must say the salesmen are very nice. They supply us with a great many vitamins and all sorts of medication in the form of free samples which Dr. Clem doles out to the needy." She led the way into the lab and slid back one of the cupboard doors above the sink. "Here they are, along with, as I warned you, the vitamins for the cut flowers and plants. Don't make a mistake and give a patient some plant food."

Cherry laughed. One bottle on the shelf was labeled *Placebo* and she knew it contained nothing but flavored sterile water. "Do we use much of that? I mean, do we have many patients who tend to be hypochondriacs?"

"Practically none," Lola replied with a grin. "Most of the people around here can't afford to be sick, let alone pretend that they are when they're not. Even very wealthy women like Mrs. Van Wyck are busy all the time with community activities: PTA meetings, the various women's clubs, the fund-raising drives for the Red Cross, the March of Dimes, the Community Chest,

Scouts, both Boys and Girls. Then there's the political situation, and the League of Women Voters is very active. Even Mrs. Nellie Carson, who consumes most of our Placebo, is so worked up over the coming election that she hasn't called us for a week. She's not really a hypochondriac. Before her husband died, she took an active part in community events and was very happy and healthy. But she's never really quite come out of mourning, though she doesn't wear black widow's weeds. The Carsons adored each other and I guess she can't reconcile herself to living alone in that big luxuriously furnished house with nobody but a slew of servants to talk to." Lola frowned. "Dr. Clem does his best, but in a way he does more harm than good. Nellie adores him almost as much as she did Mr. Carson, and is forever imagining that something is wrong with her, as an excuse for coming here or so he'll have to come see her. Last month she came in for a basal metabolism, and wouldn't you know? The stylus—the pen, you know—got stuck, so it didn't record. I called the repairman and got it fixed the same day, but Mrs. Carson is convinced that something horrible is wrong with her breathing and caused the trouble. She claims that she can't take in enough oxygen and refuses to have another test. Frankly, I'm pretty sure that it's just a game that she plays, because she's so bored with herself."

Cherry smiled. "Maybe she's the answer to the missing rebozo. Dr. Clem must be awfully fond of her if he humors her as much as you imply that he does."

"He humors her all right," Lola said with a broad

grin, "because he says that the word 'humors' originally covered all sorts of diseases, mental or physical. And he is very fond of her, but as I said before, I'm positive that he did not give her that rebozo." She gave Cherry a little push as the time clock went off. "Hie ye hence to the darkroom."

Cherry hurried off to take the film from the tank and hang it on the rack. She turned off the water and went back to the lab. "What do you think of the coming election, Lola?" she asked curiously.

"Oh, like Dr. Clem," Lola said, "I'm all for Cy, although Harry Jenner is a great guy. But, in our opinion, he's too young for the office. Sure, he'd be a new broom sweeping clean and probably accomplish a lot at first, but he's bound to make a lot of mistakes too, which would sort of cancel out his reforms, if you know what I mean."

"Lex feels more or less the same way," Cherry said thoughtfully, "but I can't help wondering why the mayor was against the new school and why the tene—"

The buzzer sounded and Lola dashed off to return in a minute with old Mr. O'Brien in tow. "Hb. Carry on." And she disappeared to answer the phone.

Inwardly Cherry shook with nervousness as she got things ready for the hemoglobin test. But Mr. O'Brien obviously was used to having a sample of his blood taken, and her confidence came back as she massaged his finger tip before swabbing it with alcohol. His face remained expressionless as she pricked his finger and sucked the drop of blood into the pipette.

While she was shaking the glass tube, he said gruffly, "Don't need a bandage for that prick," and shuffled out to the street through the lab door before Cherry could stop him.

Dr. Clem joined her then and quietly watched her work. When she had finished and handed him the written report, he said, "Good girl. You'll do."

Cherry flushed with pleasure. "Would you like me to bring the X-ray into your view box, sir?"

He shook his head. "No hurry about that. And don't call me 'sir,' Cherry Ames. Did you get your nickname because of your red cheeks?"

Cherry relaxed, smiling. "When I was in training they got me into a lot of scrapes. The Chief Resident Surgeon at Spencer kept telling me to wipe off the rouge, but of course I couldn't."

"A fine man, Dr. Wylie," Dr. Clem said. "Know him well. A bit on the strict side with interns and student nurses, but I'll bet you haven't forgotten a thing he taught you."

"I can remember practically every word he ever said," Cherry agreed. "But at first he did terrify me."

"Well, don't let me terrify you," Dr. Clem said, smiling back at her. "Now, I'm going to have a bite to eat. Then I'll go on to the Community Day Nursery. You can always reach me there at one o'clock. After that, I'll make a few house calls, but I'll keep in touch with the Answering Service. I may drop in here around two." He shrugged into his rumpled raincoat which Cherry learned later was the only topcoat he wore, except in bitter cold weather. "Did you meet Miss Marcia last night?"

"Yes, sir, I mean Dr. Clem," Cherry replied.

He stared down at her for a second, as though trying to read her mind, and then ambled out through the side door.

"Are you hungrier than I am?" Lola called from the X-ray room. "If so, go on out for lunch while I tidy up the treatment room."

Cherry was hungry but she replied, "No, you go first, Lola. I'd like to do the tidying. It'll give me a chance to get used to things before you leave me for good."

Lola appeared then in a lemon-colored rebozo which she had draped around her hair, shoulders, and arms. "Too hot for my cape now," she said, "and I'm just going across the street. Pretty, isn't it? Here, try it on."

"It's perfectly lovely," Cherry said. "I hope I get one soon, because a friend of mine promised to bring me one from Mexico City. Why, it's as soft as a baby blanket."

"That's right," Lola said. "In Mexico the women put their babies in them and carry them around slung over their backs in much the same way that the Indians carried their papooses. There are a dozen ways of wearing them. Folded, as a scarf or sash, and draped like this, with a skirt instead of a sweater or a blouse. Well, I'm off. Back soon."

Cherry wandered through the various rooms, putting things to rights and making little mental notes of questions to ask Lola. She was talking to a patient on the phone in the consultation room when the doorbell tinkled. It was too soon for Lola to come back—who could it be at this time of day? Probably a salesman, Cherry decided, and said into the mouthpiece:

"Dr. Clem may drop in around two. If he does, I'll have him call you." She hung up and hurried out to the waiting room. A tall, redheaded young man was standing there and holding a bloody handkerchief against his right temple. His lips were pale and Cherry, slipping her arm through his, said quickly:

"Come into the treatment room, sir. The doctor isn't here right now, but I'm a registered nurse and can give you first aid."

He grinned at her lopsidedly, winking blood out of his eye. "You don't look old enough to be an R.N. Where's Lola?"

"Out to lunch," Cherry said crisply. "Come on. I want you to lie down immediately."

Rather sheepishly he let her guide him into the treatment room where he stretched out on the table. Cherry deftly replaced the bloody handkerchief with a wad of sterile bandages and applied pressure. The first step always was to stop the bleeding and reassure the patient while you watched his rate of respiration.

She smiled down at him. "Your color's coming back. You look fine, but you'll look even better after I've cleaned you up." With her free hand she casually touched her fingers to his wrist. Head injuries, no matter how minor they might seem on the surface, could mean concussion or even a skull fracture. Thank goodness his pulse and respiration were normal, and since the bleeding was neither arterial nor venous, it probably would stop soon.

"Sorry I winked at you when I came in," he said with that lopsided grin. "I wasn't flirting with you, though I might at some other time."

Cherry replaced the wad of bandages with a smaller wad and said, "Hold this in place with your finger tips while I get a basin of warm water."

When she wiped away the blood which had oozed down around his right eye, he said, "Now that I can see you better I still think you look too young to be an R.N. Who are you, anyway?"

"Cherry Ames," she replied. "Dr. Clem's new nurse. Now what kind of accident were you in?"

"Accident?" he snorted. "That guy deliberately—"

"Sh-h," Cherry interrupted. "If you can't talk about it without getting excited, don't talk about it. The bleeding has stopped and we don't want it to start again."

"Okay, okay," he said rather gruffly, as he started to sit up. "Just slap on a Band-aid and I'll be on my way."

Gently but firmly Cherry pushed him back. "You're not going to leave here for quite a while. Just lie quietly while I do the talking. First I'm going to clean the area of the wound with peroxide. It effervesces, you know, and makes it easy to wipe off the dried blood . . . There. It really isn't much of a cut, but in order to guard against infection, I'll paint it with Merthiolate."

"Ow!" he grimaced. "That stings, but not as much as iodine. When I was a kid my grandmother was forever slapping iodine on my cuts. Wow! I can still hear my own yells."

Cherry laughed. "We know better nowadays. Iodine does sting like the dickens and a lot of people are allergic to it. Also, the average person is apt to keep a bottle of iodine on the shelf of his medicine cabinet until the solution gets too strong to use safely. . . . No, you're not ready to leave yet. Just relax while I decorate your forehead with a butterfly which will hold the lips of the wound together."

"Butterfly?" The young man's green eyes flashed. "Hey! what goes on? Get Dr. Clem. Where's Lola? Help!"

He looked so funny, clowning like that, that Cherry gave way to her laughter. "Help yourself," she said. "Now watch me while I make a butterfly."

He watched her suspiciously as she cut a two-inch strip from the narrow roll of adhesive. Using the sharp-pointed scissors she notched the strip in the center on both sides. Folding the tiny flaps inward, she said, "This is the only part of the bandage which will touch your wound. So we'll sterilize it by running it through the flame of a match. Will you assist in that part of this elaborate operation?"

Grinning cheerfully, he struck a match. "So that's a butterfly?"

Smiling back at him, Cherry said, "As a first-aid measure, and since the cut isn't a long one, I think one butterfly will do the trick."

"I get the idea," he said as she applied the dressing.

"The sticky part of the butterfly doesn't touch the scab on the cut. If it did, the wound might start to bleed again when the butterfly was taken off later."

"Exactly," said Cherry. "Now I'm going to check your blood pressure. That's routine with a head injury. No, please don't argue or I'll have to call Dr. Clem. If you're a friend of his, you must know that he's at the Day Nursery now and won't want to disturbed."

The young man immediately sat up, took off his jacket, and rolled up his shirt sleeve. "Wouldn't take him away from those kids for anything in the world."

Cherry donned the stethoscope, strapped the apparatus on the patient's arm and pumped it up, watching the meter. When she heard the first pulse beat through the stethoscope, she gradually let out the air, watching the meter until she heard the last beat. Then she removed the apparatus and said, "One hundred and twenty over eighty. That's normal for you, so the prognosis is good."

He rolled down his sleeve and reached for his jacket. "Say, are you an M.D. as well as an R.N.?"

"No, but I'm going to behave like one." Cherry opened the door to the small treatment room. "I'm going to order you to lie down on the couch in here until two o'clock. Dr. Clem may drop in then. In the meantime, an ice bag on your temple will help to reduce the swelling." When he obeyed orders, she added, "You've had a nasty bump. Do you want to talk about it now?" She handed him the ice bag, then covered him with a light blanket and sat on the chair beside the couch.

He sighed. "My head does sort of ache now, but I'm lucky. If it hadn't been for the steering wheel, I probably would have sailed right through the windshield. That guy ought to be arrested—forcing me to slam on my brakes like that."

His rate of respiration leaped and Cherry said, "I can't let you talk about it if you're going to get so excited. I gather that you were driving in heavy traffic and had to stop suddenly in order to avoid hitting the car in front of you. There's nothing about that to make you so angry. It happens all the time in New York City." Inwardly she was thinking, "If the wheel kept him from sailing through the windshield, he ought to have a complete exam including X-rays. I hope Dr. Clem drops in at two!"

He glared at her. "Sleepyside is not New York City and there was no traffic on the road when that guy suddenly pulled out of a side street in front of me. If anybody should ask me, I'd say that he did it deliberately. Nothing would make our beloved mayor happier than to have me laid up in a hospital for the next week or so."

Try as she did, Cherry couldn't help jumping with surprise.

He stirred restlessly. "Oh, I know you don't believe me! You think this blow on my head has affected my brain. But that's because you don't know who I am."

"I can guess," Cherry said quietly. "You're the fiery young lawyer I've been hearing so much about—Harry Jenner."

CHAPTER IX

An Unpleasant Incident

"YOU GUESSED CORRECTLY!" THE YOUNG LAWYER roared. "And I would swear under oath on the witness stand that our beloved mayor, the People's Choice, deliberately and with malice aforethought—"

"Calm down," Cherry interrupted crisply. "You're not on the witness stand; you're my patient, and if you can't talk about the accident without behaving as though you were in a courtroom, I'll leave you here alone."

She took her fingers from his pulse and he grabbed her hand. "I'll be good," he said with that crooked grin, "and you're absolutely right. I wouldn't—couldn't swear—that Cy Hillman did try to crash into me with that high-powered car of his. But if you knew anything about local politics you'd realize that my life is in danger. No, I don't really mean that," he corrected himself quickly. "To be truly honest I guess neither my life nor my limbs are in danger. Cy wouldn't dare— Or would he?"

Cherry smiled. "I can't answer that question, sir, since I don't know what you're talking about."

He chortled. "Now who's behaving as though she were in a courtroom?"

"I just want to get the facts, sir," Cherry said with a chuckle, deciding that the best way to keep this fiery patient calm was to keep him laughing.

"Very well, you shall have them," he replied. "Since there were no witnesses, and thus it would be his word against mine, it must have been an accident—a collision that missed by a hairbreadth. Please forget that I ever said anything else. But between you and me and the gatepost I will state that he's a reckless driver."

"Then," Cherry said, "I think you ought to report the accident—or whatever you want to call it—to the police."

"That would do more harm than good," he told her soberly. "The powerful minority, which is against me, would say that I cooked up the whole thing in order to defame our mayor's pure character. If I can't convince them that he's a crooked politician, how could I possibly convince them that he's a reckless driver?"

"Is he both, really and truly?" Cherry asked.

He groaned. "In my opinion, he is, but I can't get any proof that would hold up in a court of law. He is a ruthless driver, but he doesn't get involved in accidents because most people around here treat his big maroon sedan with the same respect that they treat an ambulance. They always give him the right of way, and because he *is* the mayor, the police are apt to shut their eyes on the occasions when he drives too fast. It's common courtesy for the police to do that, because he might be in a hurry on official business."

Cherry nodded. "That still doesn't make him a crooked politician."

"No," he admitted, "but the condition of those town-owned tenements does. If I could get somebody in authority to inspect them, this town would be in an uproar. But nobody pays any attention to me, and since none of the tenants dare complain, for fear of being evicted—"

"But surely," Cherry interrupted, "you have a welfare agency with a staff of social workers and visiting nurses who regularly visit people in those buildings."

"The welfare agency," he explained, "does nothing unless a complaint is registered with them. And we are woefully short of social workers and district nurses. The mayor, and he alone, *is* the housing committee, and since he won't grant me permission to examine his books and records, I can't prove what I strongly suspect: misappropriation of town funds. So all I can do is keep on making speeches which nobody in the powerful minority listens to, and keep on writing open letters to the *Sun* demanding that the mayor answer the questions which I keep on asking him. The very fact that he consistently laughs me off makes me all the more certain that he *is* guilty. If he isn't, why doesn't he follow the suggestion I made yesterday: appoint a certified public

accountant to go over the housing project's books? A
CPA's report would settle the matter in a day or so."

Suddenly Cherry remembered the wad of newspaper
which she had popped into her handbag the night before. If it was an open letter from Harry Jenner which
had made Mr. Hillman so angry, she would at least
have proof that he didn't always laugh off the young
lawyer's efforts to get elected. She started out to the desk
to get her handbag, but Lola came back then.

"Why, Harry Jenner!" Lola exclaimed in amazement.
"What on earth happened to you?"

"Hi, Lola," he said cheerfully. "I was in a slight acci-
dent. Had to stop suddenly and bumped my head.
Nothing wrong with me, except that I'm starving. Can
I go now?"

"Not until Dr. Clem has seen you," Lola said crisply.
"Run along, Cherry, and get something to eat. I'll cope
with this young man. If he really is starving, I'll give
him a cup of tea and some crackers."

When Cherry came back from lunch, Lola said, "Dr.
Clem arrived shortly after you left. He gave the patient
a thorough exam, pronounced him okay, and they both
just departed . . . after uttering words of praise for
you. How did you like Harry? Attractive, isn't he?"

"Very," Cherry said. "I couldn't help liking him.
He's got a quick temper, but he's also got a grand sense
of humor."

"He thinks you're just wonderful," Lola said.
"Couldn't stop raving about how efficient and pretty and
everything you are. Before long, you'll have all of our

patients in love with you, honey. Now, do you want to ask me some questions?"

"The most important one," Cherry replied, "is the electrocardiograph. Can you give me a refresher course?"

When Lola finished explaining about the instrument, Cherry sighed. "Oh, how I wish we had a Sally Chase to practice on. I'll never be able to remember all of those instructions."

"Pooh," said Lola, giving her a friendly hug. "You don't need a demonstration doll, Cherry. Dr. Clem usually makes the electrocardiograms himself and would want you to watch him a couple of times before he'd expect you to take over completely on your own."

"I hope so," Cherry said dubiously. "Right now, I feel sure I'd electrocute the patient."

Lola snapped her fingers. "I just had a brain storm. The Cambridge Instrument Company, which is a few miles south of here at Ossining, manufactures electrocardiographs. They'd be glad to give you a demonstration of their 'heart throb,' and let you practice on one of their employees to your heart's content. I imagine when Lex takes you sightseeing he'll show you Sing Sing Prison, so why don't you visit the Cambridge Company the same day?"

"That's a wonderful idea!" Cherry said in a relieved tone of voice. "Now could we please do some bookkeeping together? I think I understand the forms we have to fill out for patients who are covered by hospital, medical, and accident insurance, but I also saw some blanks in one of the desk drawers which seemed baffling to me."

"Workmen's Compensation probably," said Lola, taking one from the drawer. "They're really easy, because Dr. Clem fills them out in pencil. You make a typewritten copy from it and keep his penciled copy in our files."

They worked on the books and in the lab, answering the phone in between times until five thirty. Dr. Clem came in while Cherry was plugging in the sterilizer.

"How'd you girls get on?" he asked pleasantly.

"Fine," Cherry told him. "I'm not nearly as scared as I was this morning. Shall I bring you the phone messages now, Dr. Clem?"

He nodded and she brought the memos and the appointment book to him in the consultation room. "We have only three definite appointments for this evening," she said. "Mayor Hillman at seven for a checkup. Miss Lila Jones, to have her dressing changed, at seven thirty, and Mrs. Nellie Carson who wouldn't say exactly why or when she was coming."

Dr. Clem laughed. "Nellie's a grand gal and as healthy as an ox. But she's got problems—emotional problems, but not serious enough to take up the time of a busy psychiatrist. All of us country docs have patients like Nellie and we have to have patience with them. We give them what we call 'substitution therapy.' Right now, she imagines that there's something wrong with her throat, so I'll swab her tonsils and give her some of my special gargle." His heavy shoulders shook. "Gargling with salt and soda never hurt anybody and it might do her a lot of good."

"In the Hilton Clinic," Cherry said, "we saw a lot of patients with emotionally induced illnesses. E.I.I. we called it, and usually passed them on to Psychiatry."

Dr. Clem nodded again. "In this area there aren't enough psychiatrists to go around. But I don't want you to get the idea that all of my patients who have problems have imaginary illnesses. Some of them are really sick and others simply need sympathy and advice. Take Maria, for instance. There's nothing medical science can do for her, and when she first learned that she could never walk again, she didn't want to live. Then one day when I was visiting her I noticed that she was wearing a lovely shawl. She told me that it was a rebozo and that she had woven it herself on a hand loom. Gradually Ben and I encouraged her to go into the rebozo business. As soon as she found that her hands could be useful, she forgot about her legs. And now, although confined to her wheel chair, she is as spry as she ever was and as cheerful as a robin."

"I'd love to meet her," Cherry said softly.

"That's what I was leading up to," he said, his brown eyes twinkling. "First chance you get will you drop in and say hello? And while you're there, you might look over her rebozos and pick out the color which you think would be most becoming to yourself. I'd like to make you a present of one."

The bell tinkled, the phone rang, and the buzzer

sounded. The evening office hours had begun. The waiting room filled up quickly and soon it was buzzing with arguments about the coming election. When the mayor himself arrived at seven, the conversation ceased abruptly for a second, and then those who were supporting him greeted him with enthusiasm.

"Good evening, Your Honor!" cried a woman.

"Here, sit by me, Cy," an old gentleman said.

The others, who were going to vote for Harry Jenner, pretended to be so absorbed in magazines that they didn't know who had just come in. But he greeted them all with the same cordiality and good humor:

"Sorry to find you here, my friends, unless it means that, like myself, you're just calling on the doc for a routine checkup." Then he said something pleasant to each one in turn, and lightly crossed over to the desk to say to Cherry, "I'm a couple of minutes late. Hope I didn't keep Dr. Clem waiting."

"Oh, no, sir—I mean, Your Honor," Cherry said. "There were several here before you." She motioned toward an empty chair. "Won't you sit down? The doctor is just about to take some X-rays, so it'll be several minutes before he can see you."

He frowned and said in a low voice, "Well, tell him I'm here before he starts taking the pictures. *I* can't be kept waiting, you know."

Cherry forced herself to smile. "I'm sorry, Your Honor, but we're not permitted to interrupt the doctor when he's doing a fluoroscopy. But he'll be ready to see you soon. Here's the *Sun*. Wouldn't you like to—?"

Before she could say another word, he snatched up the phone, pressed the Intercom button, and sounded the buzzer. Cherry was stunned with amazement. Lola burst out of the consultation room, looking equally stunned, and darted over to the desk.

Giving Cherry a look which said plainly, "Have you lost your mind?" she gently took the phone from the mayor and said, "I'm sorry, Cy. Miss Ames is new here and she doesn't know our rules. You can't talk to Dr. Clem now."

He bowed, smiling. "Forgive me. I was misinformed. And we must forgive Miss Ames too. Any new employee, no matter how bright and pretty, is apt to make a mistake the first day or so." He subsided into the chair and picked up a magazine.

Cherry's cheeks were flaming with anger, but she knew that everyone must think that she was crimson with embarrassment. Helplessly she realized that there was nothing she could do; the old childhood rule of "Newcomer's It" would apply to anything she tried to say in her own defense. The only patient who could possibly have overheard her conversation with the mayor was the old gentleman who obviously was one of his stanchest supporters.

Lola tucked her arm through Cherry's and drew her around the corner into the lab. "It's all right, honey," she whispered. "If Dr. Clem says anything about your buzzing him at a time like that, I'll say you pressed the wrong button."

"I didn't press *any* buttons—" Cherry began, but the

bell tinkled and with a silent sigh she returned to the waiting room. This patient, with the bandaged hand, she guessed, must be Miss Lila Jones, a pretty young blonde who was the mayor's secretary. He greeted her with elaborate solicitude and escorted her to his own chair.

"Poor dear little Lila," Cherry heard him murmur loudly enough so that everyone could hear him. "I can't tell you how I have missed you at the office since that unfortunate accident robbed me of your services. That drawer in the filing cabinet must be fixed, so we can be sure that never again will it slam shut on your hand."

Lila Jones sank into the chair and looked up at him with worshipful blue eyes. "It was all my fault, Mr. Mayor. I'll never forgive myself for being so clumsy! Oh, it's too awful to think of your having to hire a substitute at a time like this when you are being unjustly attacked by your enemies. A CPA indeed!" she glanced indignantly at the patients who were on the Jenner side of the controversy. "If I hadn't been so upset by that insulting letter which that horrible man wrote to the *Sun*—"

"There, there, my dear," Mr. Hillman said soothingly. "You mustn't let things like that upset you. Learn to laugh them off as I do. Never let us forget that Mr. Jenner is a young man—a *very* young man who has no control over his temper."

"He's old enough to know when to hold his tongue," the old gentleman growled.

"He ought to be tarred and feathered," an elderly lady muttered angrily.

Just then the bell tinkled and through the glass partition of the vestibule Cherry saw that the new arrival was a plump, heavily made-up woman, wearing a black velvet hat with the largest brim Cherry had ever seen.

As the patient came into the waiting room Cherry moved forward to meet her halfway. "Mrs. Carson?"

"That's right, dearie," the woman boomed. "And who are you?"

"I'm the new nurse," Cherry said. "Miss Ames."

"Well, I declare." Mrs. Carson's face was wreathed in smiles, and the big, bright flowers on her hat bounced happily. "It's about time Clem had sense enough to hire somebody young and pretty to help Lola." Her big, black eyes traveled swiftly around the room and stopped when she caught sight of the mayor. "Oh, my stars, Cyrus Hillman, what are you doing here?"

"Good evening, Nellie," he said with a courtly bow. "You're looking prettier than ever. The very picture of health and beauty, I might say. This is a social call on the good doctor, I imagine?"

Cherry sensed that his words were tinged with faint sarcasm, and Mrs. Carson obviously felt the same way. She narrowed her eyes until the heavily mascaraed lashes meshed.

"Save your silver tongue for the folks who are going to vote for you," she said tartly. "I, for one, won't sit down in the same room with the likes of you." With that, she flounced around and swept out.

"Poor Nellie," the mayor murmured, tapping his forehead sadly. "She's never been right since her husband passed on."

Everyone began to talk at once and Cherry felt as though she were in a theater watching a play. Then Dr. Clem ushered out the patient he had just X-rayed and glanced questioningly at Cherry.

"Mrs. Dyckson is next," Cherry told him, "but Mayor Hillman phoned this morning for an appointment at seven." Mrs. Dyckson was a woman in her early thirties who, before the mayor's arrival, had stated that she was definitely going to vote for Harry Jenner.

Dr. Clem patted her on the shoulder. "In a hurry, Cora?"

She shook her head and he said, "Come along, Cy."

When the door of the consultation room closed behind them, Mrs. Dyckson said in that clear voice of hers, "Isn't that typical? There's nothing wrong with me that half an hour is going to make worse, but wouldn't you have thought that His Honor would let his secretary go in ahead of him? *Poor dear little Lila,* indeed!"

Again everyone began to talk at once and the arguments continued until the end of the office hours. Cherry tumbled into bed at ten o'clock too tired to worry about the fact that tomorrow she would be completely on her own.

CHAPTER X

Cherry Makes a Decision

TUESDAY WAS A COLD, DREARY DAY WITH THE THREAT of snow in the air, but in spite of the weather several young mothers came in with their babies who ranged from toddlers to month-old infants. Cherry was glad that one of her jobs was to keep the small fry amused while their mothers were in the consultation and treatment rooms, and she enjoyed helping Dr. Clem when he weighed the infants and gave them thorough examinations. As each mother left she thanked Cherry so warmly that Cherry glowed. At last she felt really useful and competent!

Before Dr. Clem left at twelve thirty, he said, "Theoretically, Cherry, to make it an eight-hour day, you're supposed to be off duty from two until five. You didn't take any time off yesterday, so why don't you leave at one today?" He ambled out the side door. "Just don't forget to notify the Answering Service."

Cherry tidied up the rooms, feeling blue. Where

would she spend her time off? She could have a long, leisurely luncheon and write some letters, or take a nap or go to a movie, but the very thought of eating alone was depressing. She had just finished changing into street clothes when Harry Jenner arrived.

"Hi!" He held up both hands. "I'm not here as a patient. Hoped you might have lunch with me. There's a wonderful inn on the Post Road, just south of here, where the fried chicken is really something."

"I'd love it," Cherry said, feeling as though the sun had suddenly come out. And that's just what it did when they arrived at the inn a few minutes later. By that time they were on a first-name basis and he said:

"There's an enclosed terrace in the back with a huge chimney fireplace. Let's eat out there, so you can enjoy a view of the Hudson while we eat. Some day, Cherry, I'll drive you across the Bear Mountain Bridge to West Point on the other side. We'll make a day of it. Would you like that?"

"Sounds wonderful," Cherry promptly agreed. "There are so many famous historical spots around here that I want to see. Washington Irving's home, the Headless Horseman Bridge, the Philipse Castle Restoration, and so many others that I was thinking it might be a good idea for me to rent a car during my hours off and go sightseeing by myself."

"You'd be sure to get lost," he said. "Wait until after Election Day. Then I'll show you the sights."

After he'd given the waiter their order, he added, "That is, if I'm still around by then."

Cherry stared at him. "Have you changed your mind again? Do you think your life's in danger?"

"No," he corrected her. "But I've staked everything I've got on this campaign. If I lose, it will virtually mean that the implications I've made against the mayor are false. As a result, I'll be so unpopular that I'll have to hang out my shingle some place else. I've got few enough clients as it is and none of them can afford to pay me very much."

"And you're really positive that the mayor is dishonest?" Cherry asked.

"What else can I think?" he demanded. "I know a lot of people who live in those town-owned tenements. I visited them when we were working for the new school, so I know how they live. The exteriors of those buildings are kept up, but the interiors are in deplorable shape. But unless the tenants complain or somebody in authority makes an inspection, how can I accuse the mayor of pocketing most of the housing committee funds?"

"He couldn't possibly pocket the money and get by with it," Cherry objected. "He must have to account for it to somebody like the town clerk or the supervisor."

"That's the point," Harry retorted. "He doesn't have to make an accounting to anybody. The whole project is rather extraordinary. Usually when a town takes over property for tax lien, said property is sold within a reasonable length of time. But in this case, apparently, there were no buyers and so the town became a landlord. A housing committee was formed and a maintenance fund annually allocated to it. But somewhere along the line it became a one-man committee and the only accounting that is required from him is a simple statement of total receipts and total expenditures. Since these two figures always balance perfectly, canceling each other out, nobody bothers to ask for an itemized list of rents received or for receipted bills. He's been in office for so long that the town simply takes his word for it that the tenements are a nonprofit project, run solely for the benefit of the poor. Whereas," he finished exasperatedly, "exactly the opposite is obviously true. People are packed in like sardines, the stairs are on the verge of collapse, the plumbing is a disgrace, and nothing has been painted for at least ten years. The fire escapes are okay because they can be seen from the street."

"How horrible!" Cherry frowned. "If what you say is true, I can't understand how such a man ever got into office."

"That's what I've been trying to discover," Harry told her. "Every spare minute I have I spend in the *Sun's* morgue combing the files for a clue. The editor in chief, Bob Lindsay, is one of my oldest friends; his father owns the paper, but of course they can't take sides in the election without disastrous results to their circulation. However, Bob has given me free access to their files, even though he knows that I'm searching for something shady in the mayor's past. I've examined all of the clippings in the envelopes labeled Cyrus R. Hillman, and I can't find anything derogatory. My guess is that he started out as an honest man, then something happened which made him stray from the straight and narrow path."

"Does he live beyond his salary?" Cherry asked. "I mean, is he an extravagant person?"

"No." Harry groaned. "That's one of the things that weakens my feeble attack. Except for that high-powered car of his, he has no expensive tastes; lives very simply, in fact, and is a bachelor with no dependents. Like myself, he was an only child. His parents died when he was a boy and he was brought up by grandparents, long deceased. So far as I can see, the only obligations he possibly could have would be to people who boosted him up the political ladder in the early days of his career, and those obligations must have been paid off ages ago in the form of appointments and/or contracts."

"I understand," Cherry said, "that he accuses you of that kind of—well, bribery. Doesn't he claim that if you are elected you will have completely unnecessary improvements made by contractors who are working to get you elected?"

Harry nodded. "He also accuses me of making mountains out of molehills and a lot of people believe him, because a lot of people think that the new school was completely unnecessary. They argue that what was good enough for them should be good enough for the younger generation, completely overlooking the fact that our population has leaped appallingly in the last ten years. The sad part of it is that the apartments and homes that have been built to absorb this influx from big cities are not in the low-rent bracket, so it is a fact that the people who live in those tenements have no place else to live. But that's no excuse for the conditions that exist."

"In the beginning," Cherry said thoughtfully, "there must have been a secretary on the committee who submitted an accounting to the town supervisor. Have you examined those records?"

"That's right," he said, "and I strongly suspect that there was mishandling of funds way back then. You're an office nurse, Cherry. You know how easy it would be for you to cheat Dr. Clem."

Cherry giggled. "I'm not that good at bookkeeping."

He grinned that lopsided grin. "Listen. Suppose I owe Dr. Clem fifty dollars and decided to pay it off by dropping in every now and then and giving you ten dollars. What's to prevent you from pocketing one of those payments? You don't give patients receipts for cash payments, do you?"

"Yes, we do," Cherry said firmly. "For their income-tax records, if for no other reason."

He chuckled. "You got me that time. Let's take it this way. Suppose he gives you fifty dollars to pay some bills. What's to prevent you from pocketing some of it."

"Dr. Clem pays all of the bills himself," she told him. "One of my jobs is to make out the checks for him around the first of the month for the towel service and things like that, with stamped, addressed envelopes. But he signs and mails the checks himself. As a matter of fact, he gets very few bills, because of that barter system of his, you know."

Harry groaned. "I should never have tried to use you and Dr. Clem as an example. But you know what I'm driving at, Cherry. The mayor could have obtained money from the committee's treasurer and accounted for it with phony receipted bills. And as for cash expenditures, why the sky was the limit! In the records there are an awful lot of petty-cash vouchers signed by the mayor, who was, apparently, from the very beginning the only active member of the committee. The others were just names who gradually dropped out of the picture. According to those vouchers, he paid enormous sums in cash for labor and materials, which struck me as odd. Normally work of that kind is done by a contractor who presents a bill when the job is finished and is paid by check. I asked His Honor about that at a public meeting once and he virtually patted me on the head and gave me a lollipop. Said that when I grew up I'd learn that public officials are morally obligated at all times to save the town's money. Claimed that by hiring independent laborers and supplying them with materials he eliminated the graft, which, he added pointedly, so often occurs when big contractors enter the picture. He sat down, laughing, amid loud applause."

"He doesn't always laugh you off," Cherry said, and took the crumpled ball of newspaper from her handbag. "Whatever this is, it made him so mad that he ripped it from the paper, crushed it into this wad, and hurled it out of a booth at the coffee shop. I happened to be watching his reflection in the mirror behind the counter and out of curiosity picked up the ball. I haven't looked at it, but I'll bet it's that open letter of yours which appeared on the front page of last Sunday's *Sun*."

Harry smoothed the page out on the tablecloth. "It is," he said exultantly. "So I do get under His Honor's skin occasionally?"

"He gets under my skin," Cherry said tartly, and told him what had happened at the office the evening before. "I'll never forgive him for putting me in a position like that! He had no business picking up the phone in the first place, and then to let everyone think that *I* had buzzed the doctor!"

They ate in silence for a while, then Harry said, "Cherry, you can't vote in the coming election, so you're more or less neutral. But will you help me? Dr. Clem told me yesterday that you've got quite a reputation for tracking down mysteries."

"I'd love to help you," Cherry said. "But how can I?"

"It'll be a long, hard job," he said, "but with two of us working I think we could get somewhere pretty fast. I have an idea that if we could go through the back numbers of the *Sun* and trace the mayor's career back, step by step, to the time when he first held a public office, we might come across something which would give him a motive for stealing town funds."

"But you've already examined the clippings in his file at the *Sun*," Cherry objected.

"I know," he admitted, "but they're incomplete for some reason. The dates which were stamped on the old clips are so faded that I can't read them, and anyway,

I don't think we can expect to get a clue from any one news item. We'll probably have to draw our conclusions from a combination or chain of events."

"I think you'd better turn the job over to the FBI," Cherry said when the waiter had brought coffee and ice cream. "It would take us a century to go through all of the back numbers for twenty-five years."

Harry shrugged. "You forget that the *Sun* is a small-town paper, consisting of five or six sheets, and up until recently was published only once a week. I've already gone back ten years and it didn't take very long." He leaned forward, his green eyes pleading. "I wouldn't have asked you to help, Cherry, if Dr. Clem and Lex hadn't told me that you were interested in solving crimes."

"But we don't even know that a crime was committed," Cherry argued. "However, I'd still like to help. When do we start?"

"Right now," he said. "You're off duty until five, aren't you?"

She nodded. "And unless we're awfully busy, I can leave this evening around eight thirty. Frankly, I'd rather spend my evenings in a newspaper morgue than in that morgue I'm living in." She shivered. "It gives me the creeps—makes me imagine things. The first night I thought I heard someone weeping. The next morning when I met Mrs. Briggs I got the feeling that she was my enemy. All plain foolishness."

"The weeping," he said, "could have been creaking floor boards, but I've got news for you. Briggs and

Coombs hate everybody except Miss Marcia. All three of them hate pretty young women. So if things get too tough, I'll scout around and try to find some other place for you to stay. If Granny were alive, she'd have wanted you to stay with us. I had to sell the house, you know, in order to pay my law school expenses." He paid the check and they went out to his car. As they drove north, he added, "Granny would have loved this fight I'm having with Hillman. She never did like him. It's funny, because most of the old-timers, as well as his own contemporaries, are on his side."

"I gather," Cherry said, "that Mrs. Nellie Carson despises him, and they're about the same age."

"That's right," Harry agreed. "Eight years ago her husband ran for mayor and was defeated by Hillman. I gathered from the back numbers of the *Sun* that during the campaign Hillman did a bit of mild mudslinging which Mr. Carson bitterly resented. I hoped to find that he'd retaliated in kind, which might have given me a lead to something shady in His Honor's past, but Nellie's husband was evidently too much of a gentleman to stoop to such methods."

Cherry chuckled. "But you're not?"

He roared with laughter. "There's a vast difference between mudslinging and exposing facts." He turned into a side street and parked. "Well, here we are at the *Sun's* offices. Let's hope we find something."

"I hope so," Cherry said thoughtfully. "I've made up my mind, Harry. I don't like the mayor and I'll do everything I possibly can to help you win the election."

CHAPTER XI

Another Accident

BUT THEY HAD NO LUCK, ALTHOUGH THEY SEARCHED through several big binders of back numbers. Harry drove Cherry back to Dr. Clem's at five o'clock and came in with her. "I forgot that I'm supposed to have my wound looked at, nurse," he said, grinning.

Cherry went straight to the phone and called the Answering Service. When she finished taking the messages, she told Harry, "Dr. Clem won't be in until shortly before six."

"I'll wait," he said, unzipping the brief case he had brought in with him. "Then I'll be sure to be the first patient."

Cherry went into the dressing room and changed back into uniform. She had just donned her cap when the bell tinkled and immediately afterward she heard Harry shout:

"Wow, Tommy! What happened to you?"

Cherry hurried out to the waiting room. A thin, teen-age boy, with the help of the young lawyer, was hopping in from the vestibule. One pant leg of his dungarees was torn and around his knee was a bloody, makeshift bandage.

"Bring him right into the treatment room, Harry," Cherry said, leading the way. When the boy was stretched out on the table, she removed the tail of his shirt which he had tied around his knee and replaced it with a wad of sterile bandages.

"This is Miss Cherry Ames, Tommy," Harry was saying. "She's Dr. Clem's new nurse. She'll fix you up fine. I was her patient yesterday and she's good, but good."

The boy grinned. "Hello, Miss Cherry. I'm Tommy Regan. You probably know my mother. She cleans for Dr. Clem."

Cherry smiled at him. "I haven't met her yet, Tommy, but I hope to soon. How'd you bang your knee?"

The grin on his freckled face fled and he scowled darkly. "That guy! He drives too darn fast. I hate him! I hate him!" He raised his head and shoulders, resting on his elbows. "I was biking along my paper route, minding my own business, when all of a sudden he comes roaring along. If I hadn't pulled over into the ditch, he would have run over me. They ought to take his license away from him."

Cherry cut away the remnants of the pant leg and cleaned the area of the wound.

"I'd report him to the police," Tommy continued, "'cept I don't dare, on account of Mom."

"Bring him into the treatment room, Harry," Cherry said.

"I gather," Harry put in, "that you're talking about our mayor?"

Tommy's blue eyes flashed. "I'm not saying anything, Harry Jenner. I don't know who was driving that big red sedan, and I didn't get the license number, so don't ask me any more questions."

Harry tapped him lightly on the chin with his fist. "You're among friends, son. I got this thing on my head because of the same guy, and Miss Cherry is on our side. Besides, she's a nurse and has taken an oath never to give away anything secret she hears from patients."

"That's right," Cherry added. "Now, I'm going to paint this cut with Merthiolate, and I guess you know it'll sting a bit."

"Pooh." Tommy winced slightly. "That didn't hurt at all." But tears welled up in his eyes.

"Why, Tommy," Harry said, "it didn't hurt that much, did it? I never saw you cry before."

"That's not why he's crying." Cherry put her arms around the boy. "He's crying because he had a bad fright. It's not much fun almost getting run over."

The boy closed his eyes tightly and he shook his head. "I'm crying 'cause I'm mad. That guy—! Mom's scared of him. And he didn't want us to have a new school. If he had to go to a school that was so crowded you couldn't hardly learn anything, he'd know what it was like. Mom says he's just forgotten, 'cause the schools weren't crowded when he was a boy, but he knows just the same. Most of the time you can't get into the library to borrow a book or look up something, 'cause it's the music room too. And we don't have shop and the girls don't have cooking and when you want to ask the teacher a question she's too busy 'cause there are too many kids, and—and I've just gotta learn a lot 'cause I'm going to be a newspaperman some day, just like Mr. Lindsay!"

"Don't worry about anything," Harry said gently. "Everything's going to be all right. You'll go to high next year and it's not quite so crowded as the grade school. And you've made a good start toward being a reporter. Tommy," he told Cherry, "is the *Sun's* all-star distributor. He's won the award of a twenty-five-dollar savings bond ten times since he was given a route. When he's old enough to get working papers he's going to night school and get a job as a copy boy on the *Sun.* Isn't that the scheme you and Bob Lindsay cooked up, Tommy?"

The boy nodded. "But how am I going to bike with this knee? It's not bleeding now, but if I bend it, it will."

"Don't worry about that, either," Cherry said soothingly. "Dr. Clem will be here pretty soon and he'll fix you up so your knee will get well soon. Haven't you a friend who can take your place in the meantime?"

"Sure," he said more cheerfully. "My cousin Mike O'Brien. He used to have a route, but he's kind of lazy. He won't get any new customers, so I won't win another bond."

"Hey," Harry interrupted, "you can't expect to win the award every single time."

"I guess not," Tommy admitted with a slow smile. "Is it right what you said, Harry? Is Miss Cherry on our side, honest and truly?"

"I'll speak for myself." Cherry plugged in the sterilizer. "I'm not on the side of the man who almost ran over you."

"Okay," he went on, "then I'll tell you two something, but you gotta promise never to let anyone know I told you."

"We promise," Cherry and Harry said in unison.

"It's like this," the boy began. "Something funny is going on. You know that old ramshackle house out on Bullethole Road?"

Harry nodded. "Bullethole Road," he told Cherry, "is well-named. It's only about a mile long, is full of ruts, and there's only one house on it—a sort of shack. Nobody ever uses the road, except when in a hurry. It's a short cut from the avenue to the parkway. Now go on, Tommy."

"Well," the boy continued, "a man named Bostwick bought the shack last summer and right off I got him for a customer. It's the last house on my route, so on collection day, which is the first of the month, I always get there late. Around six instead of five thirty. And you know what? Every single time I get to Bullethole Road around six o'clock, I pass the may— I mean that big red sedan, which is parked about midway between Mr. Bostwick's mailbox and where the road begins. And after I leave Mr. Bostwick's paper and collect from him and start back, there are two cars there, and one of them is a New York City taxi."

"That *is* strange," Harry murmured. "How often have you noticed this—this meeting, Tommy?"

He counted on his fingers. "First of August, first of September, and first of October. And I'll betcha if you go out there around six o'clock on the first of November, you'll see what I saw."

Harry glanced at Cherry. "I think I'll do just that. Did you ever see who was in the taxi, Tommy?"

"Sure," he said. "Before I get to where the two cars are parked, the taxi always passes me on the way to the parkway. There's nobody in that taxi but the driver. When I get to the spot where the two cars were parked the may— Oh, heck, the *mayor's* car has already started back toward the avenue, so I can't see if there's somebody else in it but His Honor. But when I pass it on my way to Bostwick's, there's nobody else in it."

"But he might have picked up a passenger from the taxi?" Harry asked.

"I wouldn't know about that," the boy replied. "On account of the bend in the road, I can't see the cars when I'm on Mr. Bostwick's porch, collecting from him."

"There are two bends in that narrow road," Harry explained to Cherry. "And from what Tommy has told us I gather that the cars meet at a point between the two bends. So it follows that Mr. Bostwick couldn't see them and neither could anybody passing along the avenue. The conclusion I draw from those facts leads me to believe that the mayor does not wish to be seen."

"That's right," Tommy said. "I don't think he paid any mind to me the first couple of times I saw them, but the last time maybe he did, and I was thinking that maybe—maybe that's why he tried to run over me a while ago."

Cherry gasped. "You mustn't think that, Tommy. Nobody would be so ruthless—so horribly cruel."

"I guess not," the boy admitted. "Maybe he just wanted to scare me. And he did scare me. I'm not crazy about the idea of going out to Bostwick's on the first of next month. If he forced me off the road, I wouldn't just fall into a ditch. I'd go off the embankment and get hurt real bad."

"That'll never happen," Harry cut in decisively. "You see, Cherry, on the north side of Bullethole Road there's sort of a ravine. It's not a sheer drop, but the land does slope rather abruptly down to the gully. There should be a fence on that side of the road, but there isn't. As a matter of fact, when Nellie Carson's husband was running for mayor he made an issue of that ravine. Said that the town should build a stone wall there because any driver who lost control of his car while traveling around those bends wouldn't have a prayer. It was then that Mr. Hillman started slinging mud. He claimed that Mr. Carson simply wanted to get money from the town for other purposes; that the road was never used; and that Mr. Carson had been gambling heavily in Wall Street and was on the verge of losing his fortune."

Harry shrugged. "The implication was obvious, in view of the fact that our mayor can get funds from the town without an accounting. But the truth of the matter is that Mr. Carson did not lose his fortune, and that road hasn't even got caution markers, although it is used quite frequently as a short cut."

"I don't understand why the mayor can get funds without having to account for them," Cherry said. "In Hilton the town supervisor is the chief executive and also acts as treasurer, but he has to account for every penny he spends."

"That's the way it should be," Harry agreed. "Most towns don't have a mayor—the supervisor is the boss. But when Honest Cy's term as town supervisor was about to expire, the board, influenced by him undoubtedly, decided to adopt the town-manager plan. He was elected by an overwhelming majority and has been in office ever since. The town manager, or mayor as we call him, is the administrative head of the government, with much more power than the supervisor had. In the case of Sleepyside, it amounts in some ways almost to a dictatorship. If I'm elected, a lot of those powers are going to be rescinded."

"I hope you are elected, Harry," Tommy chimed in. "Practically everybody I know is for you, though most of them don't dare say so."

Harry sighed. "The trouble is that a lot of people who *are* for me won't dare *vote* for me. They don't understand the machines—I can't make them believe that the balloting is completely secret."

The bell tinkled, the phone rang, and Dr. Clem came in all at the same moment. He took a quick look at Tommy's knee and decided that it would need a couple of sutures. Then he examined Harry's wound and dismissed him with:

"Run along, lad. And don't be surprised if you wake up tomorrow morning with a beautiful black eye. Drop in again toward the end of the week and we'll take off Cherry's butterfly."

"See you at eight thirty," said Harry to Cherry as he left.

Cherry got the instruments ready on a sterile towel and assisted the doctor while he gave Tommy a local anesthetic and sewed the lips of the cut together.

"Now, sonny," Dr. Clem said as he helped Tommy get off the table, "you can walk, stiff-legged. Those splints will keep you from bending your knee even when you're asleep." He turned to Cherry. "It's quite a piece from here to where Tommy lives. Here are my car keys. Would you like to drive the boy home?"

"Naw, she doesn't have to do that," Tommy protested. " 'Sides, I got my bike and paper bag out in front. We couldn't put my bike in your sedan, Dr. Clem. I can walk it home."

"Don't worry about the bike, Tommy," Cherry said quickly. "I'm sure Harry will be glad to take it to you this evening in his convertible. I'll run out and get the bag now and come right back for you."

Five minutes later, with Tommy in the back seat

giving directions, Cherry turned off the Post Road into a narrow cobblestoned street which was lined on both sides with sturdy-looking, old-fashioned red-brick buildings. Even though it was twilight, Cherry could see that they were in good condition and that the fire escapes were modern. She couldn't help wondering if perhaps Harry Jenner had been exaggerating when he described the interiors.

"It's the next one on your right," Tommy called, and Cherry slowed to a stop. "We live in the basement. My mother's the super, you see. We don't pay any rent and that's why— Never mind," he interrupted himself as she helped him out of the car. "I can get down the steps myself. Thanks, Miss Cherry."

"I'd rather see you safely inside," Cherry protested. "You're not used to walking stiff-legged yet, Tommy. Besides, I'd like to meet your mother."

He closed his eyes tightly, swallowed hard, and shook his sandy head. "No, please. Mom wouldn't like it. Not unless I told her first that you were coming."

"I understand," Cherry said sympathetically, thinking, "The poor woman probably is so busy taking care of the whole house that she hasn't time to keep her own apartment tidy." Aloud she said: "I won't go inside. I'll just help you down the steps."

"No, you don't understand," he blurted in a hoarse whisper. "There are five of us and we only have three rooms. Mom keeps them just as clean as she can with no hot water, and the cement walls and floors so damp and moldy. But there's no place out in back where she can hang the clothes on washday, so—so" his voice ended in a sob.

Cherry caught her breath, very close to tears herself. She had seen attractive basement apartments in Greenwich Village, but the Regan family was obviously living in an honest-to-goodness cellar.

"And it's all his fault," Tommy went on stormily but quietly. "We used to own this building, and we had a big, sunny apartment on the second floor. Then Dad got hit by that freight car and Mom was awful sick for a couple of years after Dottie was born. At least I remember that Mike's mother took care of us, and the next thing I remember was when we had to move down to the cellar because we couldn't pay the taxes." He sniffed. "Everyone said the mayor was real nice not to throw us out on the street and to let Mom have the janitor's job. Yeah, real nice, he was. Real nice!"

He broke away from Cherry and limped down the short flight of steps. Cherry stared after him until he disappeared in the gloom. So the mayor packed people like sardines into the town-owned tenements. So he hired women to do men's work. So he forced families into dank cellars!

"All of that," Cherry said to herself decisively, "has got to stop. No matter what happens Mr. Cyrus Hillman must not be re-elected!"

CHAPTER XII

A Search at Night

"I HEARTILY AGREE WITH YOU," HARRY SAID TO CHERRY that evening as they ate dinner in a booth at the coffee shop, "but there isn't anything anyone can do. Those tenements do exist in violation of both health and fire regulations, but the tenants won't complain about anything. Nobody else is interested—they accept the mayor's statements that everything is just fine. I reported those buildings myself, but the commissioners didn't take me seriously. I'm a new broom sweeping clean; I'm a troublemaker; when I accuse the mayor of gross neglect I'm trying to defame his pure character so that I can defeat him on Election Day."

His broad shoulders drooped disconsolately. "Even my best friend, Bob Lindsay, won't back me up. He says he would commit circulation suicide and/or invite a libel suit if he published my statements without the authorization of the health and fire commissioners. He does publish my letters on the front page, and has been criticized for doing so, but that's all he dares to do."

"But there must be some way of correcting the ghastly situation," Cherry argued. "Isn't there a housing regulation against packing people in like sardines?"

He shook his head. "Those buildings were erected during the Victorian era of high ceilings. The town code sets four hundred cubic feet of space per person as the minimum—*cubic* feet, mind you, so with ceilings twelve feet high the mayor *can* legally pack 'em in like sardines." He clenched his hands. "That's another law that's going to be changed if I'm elected. It's so obvious that the requirement should be based on a square-footage basis I can't understand why someone didn't propose an amendment ages ago." He shrugged. "Maybe somebody did and the mayor saw to it that the proposition was defeated before it was put to a vote."

Cherry sighed. "You've just got to win, Harry. Let's skip dessert and go to work."

They spent the rest of the evening laboriously scanning back numbers of the *Sun*. And from then on, whenever both of them were free, they worked together. Harry was busy a lot of the time with campaign speeches, and on Thursday he gave several talks over the air at the local broadcasting station. That afternoon, as had been prearranged, Lex stopped for Cherry as soon as the morning office hours ended, and they drove south along the winding river road to have lunch at the Tappan Hill Restaurant in Tarrytown.

As they admired the view of the river, Lex said, "That's the Tappan Zee, one of the widest and most lakelike sections of the Hudson. Some day when we have more time we'll visit all of the interesting historic spots in the Tarrytowns."

"The Tarry*towns?*" Cherry asked.

Lex nodded. "Sleepy Hollow Land, as it's called, includes three Hudson River Valley towns: North Tarrytown, Tarrytown, and Irvington."

After lunch they drove north again to Ossining where Cherry was given a chance to practice with an electrocardiograph until she felt sure that she had mastered the technique. Then they surveyed the grim walls of the state prison.

"How on earth did Sing Sing get such a pretty name?" Cherry wanted to know.

"Originally," Lex explained, "this part of the Hudson was occupied by Sintsink Indians of the Mohegan tribe. Gradually it became known as Sing Sing, and the name has stuck to the penitentiary, although the town received the name of Ossining around the middle of the nineteenth century." He glanced at his watch. "I'm due at the hospital at six, so we'd better get going."

On Wednesday Cherry had found her uniforms waiting for her at the post office and on Friday morning there was a package from Wade which had been mailed from New York the day before. Cherry opened it in the office and was delighted to discover that it contained a lovely, soft salmon-pink rebozo. The weather had turned warm again and she decided to wear it when she was off duty that afternoon, instead of the cardigan sweater she had donned that morning. Friday was always a busy day for Dr. Clem, so it was after two when Cherry crossed the street to meet Harry for lunch at the coffee shop.

The moment Ben caught sight of her he cried out, "Oh, you're wearing one of Maria's rebozos! Did the doctor give it to you?"

"No," Cherry told him. "A friend of mine who's a pilot brought it back from Mexico City."

Ben leaned across the counter to examine the tassels. "I could have sworn that it was the one Maria made last year for Dr. Clem. When you go up to say hello to her, Miss Cherry, I'll bet you she says the same thing."

Sure enough, when Cherry entered the sunny room on the second floor, the sweet-faced woman clapped her hands with pleasure. "I am so flattered, Señorita Cher-ree. You are wearing a Maria rebozo. The good doctor geeve it to you for being such a good nurse, yes?"

"No." Cherry smiled and explained.

Maria reached into the straw basket which hung from one arm of her wheel chair and produced several tiny balls of fine yarn. "These are what you call leftovers," she said, "and you can see, señorita, that the *rosada* one is exactly the same color."

"It's true," Cherry admitted. "What a coincidence!"

"I remember the color very well," Maria continued, "because by Lola it was so much admired. I thought without doubt that the good doctor would geeve it to her for Christmas, but no. Such a disappointment for *la pobre* Lola! I would make her one equal, but when I write to my seester for more yarn, there is no more."

"The lemon-colored one the doctor did give her," Cherry said quickly, "is very becoming. Well, I must go now, Maria. I'll drop in again this evening."

Because it was still warm after evening office hours, Cherry decided to leave her cardigan in the office closet permanently and wore her rebozo again. "We're due for a sudden cold snap," she reflected, "and it'll be nice to have a sweater handy."

Harry was in a very depressed mood when he arrived. "We're getting nowhere, Cherry. I've been thinking that we ought to skip the financial, society, sports, and real-estate sections, and there couldn't be anything on the women's page of interest."

"I'm not so sure of that," Cherry objected. "Let's don't skip any pages. But I do think that we may have started at the wrong end. Perhaps we should begin at the time when Mr. Hillman first became mayor—or even before that. I've been carefully reading that little feature on the editorial pages which is titled Ten Years Ago Today, and I discovered this evening that Mr. Hillman started out as councilman and was town supervisor before he became mayor."

"So what?" Harry demanded impatiently. "I told you all about how he leaped from supervisor to mayor."

"I know," Cherry said, "but I can't help wondering if maybe something happened around that time which may have changed him from an honest politician to an overly ambitious one. Some little thing . . ."

"You're absolutely right," Harry interrupted. "Let's

go back to when he first entered politics—a quarter of a century ago, and work forward."

But they were doomed to disappointment. When they asked for the binders containing those editions of the *Sun*, the elderly clerk shook his head and said:

"There was no such thing as the *Sun* twenty-five years ago. It was founded twenty years ago last May by Mr. Lindsay's father."

"You're crazy, Joe," Harry retorted impatiently. "I can remember reading comic strips in the *Sun* when I was a kid."

"Not the *Sun*, Mr. Jenner," the clerk replied. "It was the *Bugle* in those days. When it folded, Mr. Lindsay bought it and changed the name."

"Well, get me the *Bugle* files then," Harry said. "Time's awastin', Joe."

The old man shook his head again. "They're not here, Mr. Jenner. When we moved to this new building, they were put in storage."

Harry stared at him in amazement. "Do you mean to tell me, Joe, that Bob Lindsay is such a fool that he put the entire *Bugle* morgue in storage? Why, the clips are almost as important a part of a newspaper as the presses."

"That's right," the clerk agreed, "and the clips aren't in storage. When we moved, they were refiled by a bunch of morons who threw out hundreds of envelopes which they didn't think were worth saving. We caught on to them by the time they got to the J's, and Mr. Lindsay Sr. had a stroke when he heard about it. Anyway, what's in storage are the binders containing the *Bugle* from the day it was founded until the day it folded. Every now and then the reporters have to go to the warehouse to look up something and they just about have a stroke when they do. It's a filthy place with no electricity, and the paper is so old it practically crumbles when you turn the pages."

"Wow!" Harry glanced at Cherry. "Do you still want to go back a quarter of a century or shall we quit right now?"

"I'd love to see those old editions," Cherry replied.

"Be back in a minute." Harry hurried off and returned in five minutes with a slip of paper which he waved at Cherry. "Our Open sesame for the night watchman. Come on, Cinderella, it'll be eleven o'clock before we know it if we don't hurry."

He stopped at a drugstore to buy two flashlights, and then drove on through the tenement district down to the wharf. The warehouse was a sturdy-looking but weather-beaten building with black windows. Harry knocked on the door and then pounded it with both fists. "The old guy's kind of deaf," he told Cherry. "Also, he's pretty badly crippled with arthritis, so he moves at a snail's pace. Tim O'Brien is his name. Maybe you've met him. He's a patient of Dr. Clem's."

"I have," Cherry said. There was a rattle of heavy keys and the door slowly opened inward. "Good evening," she said to the bent, white-haired old man who was standing there with a lantern in one hand and a bunch of keys in the other.

"Hi, Tim," Harry said cheerfully. "Miss Cherry and I want to look at the old *Bugle* files."

"Can't let you in there without a permit," Mr. O'Brien said sourly. "Only reporters allowed in that room and they have to have written permits."

"Well, here's ours," Harry said. "Which room is it, Tim? On this floor or upstairs?"

The old man raised the lantern and read the piece of paper carefully, so carefully that it seemed to Cherry that he must be trying to memorize every word on it. At last he gestured with his thumb. "Up the stairs, first door on your right."

Cherry and Harry pressed the buttons on their flashlights and hurried off. Halfway up the steep stairs they realized that Tim O'Brien was slowly following them, muttering to himself:

"Always in a hurry, these young people. Waste a lot of breath that way. What's the use of their leaping up like mountain goats? The door's locked and I got the key."

"Oh, no," Harry moaned. "At this rate it'll be eleven o'clock before we even see a binder." They continued up to the top and waited impatiently. "I wish you lived somewhere else," Harry complained, "so you could stay out until midnight occasionally. Tomorrow night for instance. You can sleep late on Sunday mornings."

"Not this Sunday," Cherry said. "I'm going to spend the day in New York with my friends."

"Oh, no, you're not!" he yelled. "You promised to help me. Election Day is a week from next Tuesday."

"I know," Cherry said thoughtfully, "and I do want to help all I can, Harry. But I have a date with Lex to-morrow night, and I promised the girls that I'd come in on Sunday to bring back the uniforms they loaned me."

"Mail them back," he retorted. "And as for Lex, break the date. Why, going out with a doctor would be as bad as a postman taking a walk on his holiday."

Cherry laughed. "I *could* mail the uniforms back, but I can't break the date with Lex. He'd have a fit."

"Let him have a fit," Harry snorted. "He's a doctor, so he knows how to unfit himself."

Tim O'Brien was unlocking the door now and they started inside. "Just a minute, just a minute," he grumbled. "You forgot to sign the book. It's on a stand down by the door. And don't forget to sign out when you leave."

Down they went, hand in hand, signed their names with the exact time of their arrival and dashed back up again. "That guy!" Harry muttered when at last they were alone in the musty, dusty storeroom. "He'll drive me crazy before he's through." He played the beam of his torch along the cobwebby walls which were lined with shelves. "Gosh, there must be a thousand binders here and the dates on the spines are so faded and dirty I can't read them, can you?"

"We'll have to do some dusting first, I'm afraid," Cherry said, "but with what?"

Harry took a handkerchief from the pocket of his jacket and gave it to her; then he took another from his hip pocket. "Well, here goes."

Cherry tied her rebozo around her waist and rolled up the sleeves of her blouse. They worked in silence for a while, then Cherry cried excitedly, "I think I'm on the right shelf, Harry! This date looks like June or July twenty-five years ago."

He peered over her shoulder. "You're right!" Then he yanked the big binder out and groaned, "Oh, I give up! How can we work without a table?"

"We'll just have to kneel on the floor," Cherry said cheerfully. "This skirt is due for the cleaner's soon, anyway. How about your suit?"

"It's my other one," he said ruefully, "but I'll sacrifice it for such a good cause. No wonder those reporters hate to be sent over here. I'll bet they hand in a big expense account when they come back."

Cherry opened the cover and played the beam of her flashlight on the yellowed front page. The word *Hillman* seemed to leap out of the headline on the right-hand column:

COUNCILMAN HILLMAN
WILL RUN FOR
TOWN SUPERVISOR

Harry took another binder from the shelf and knelt beside her. "Anything exciting?"

"Just this," Cherry said, pointing to the headline. "But we already knew that."

"Read every line in the story," he cautioned her. "There might be a clue somewhere."

They worked until ten thirty, and although the editions in both binders were packed with accounts of Cyrus Hillman, the councilman who was running for town supervisor, they found no clues. As they drove back toward Main Street, Cherry said wearily, "If my hands and face are as dirty as yours, I think I'd better wash up before I appear at The Manor. Coombs would take one look and slam the door in my face."

He glanced at her sidewise. "You look cute with that smudge on your nose and those cobwebs in your hair, but I doubt if Miss Marcia's major-domo would think so. We can stop off at the coffee shop and—"

Just then the clock in the Town Hall tower began to strike. Instead of striking once to show the quarter hour, it kept on going. Cherry emitted a faint scream. "My watch must be slow. Oh, Harry, it's already eleven o'clock. What'll I do?"

He stepped on the accelerator. "We'll be there in three minutes." But the light at the intersection turned red at that very moment, so it was eight minutes past eleven when they raced up the steps to The Manor's front porch.

Harry lifted the knocker and let it go with a bang. "They have no right to be so fussy," he grumbled. "Calm down, Cherry. If they don't open the door, I'll break it down."

Cherry giggled nervously. "You'd need a battering ram. It's made of solid oak beams."

And then the door opened and Coombs appeared. "Good evening, Miss Ames," he said coldly. "I was just about to retire. This is most unusual. Most unusual. I shall have to report the matter to Miss Charlton."

"Ah, cut it, Coombs," Harry interrupted. "What's a few minutes between friends? Miss Ames was late because she's been working for me."

The old butler raised his eyebrows disapprovingly. "Indeed? I was under the impression, Master Harry, that she had been engaged by Dr. Brown." He moved slightly and Cherry quickly slipped inside.

"Good night, Harry," she whispered as the butler closed the door.

"There is no need to whisper now," Coombs informed her icily. "The knocker has already disturbed everyone in the East Wing, as well as Miss Charlton. The acoustics in this house are rather peculiar, miss."

"I'm sorry," Cherry said contritely. "It won't happen again."

"I should think not!" Miss Marcia suddenly appeared in the doorway which opened into her private section of the house. She was wearing an old-fashioned purple flannel wrapper with a high neck and long sleeves, and her hair flowed around her shoulders. She beckoned to Cherry. "Do me the kindness, Miss Ames, of coming into my apartment and explaining your behavior."

Cherry meekly followed her into what was the most charming room she had ever seen. But she had only time for one admiring glimpse before Miss Marcia closed the door, snatched the rebozo from her shoulders, and cried out:

"You thief. You common little thief!"

CHAPTER XIII

Clues at Last

FOR A MINUTE CHERRY WAS SO SURPRISED THAT SHE couldn't move.

"Now get out!" Miss Marcia's voice was taut with anger. "Pack your belongings and get out."

"But, Miss Marcia," Cherry protested bewilderedly, "I was only eight minutes late. Is that such a crime?"

"Don't speak to me." Miss Marcia pointed to the door. "You're fortunate that I don't intend to report this to the police."

Cherry's cheeks burned and she felt hot all over with rage. "The police? You must be insane, Miss Marcia. I'll be very glad to leave. Just give me my rebozo—"

"*Your* rebozo?" The angry woman shook the shawl under Cherry's nose. "Why, you common little thief. How dare you?"

Cherry drew herself up proudly. "It *is* my rebozo. A friend of mine brought it back from Mexico City. Now please give it to me at once—or *I'll* call the police."

Miss Marcia's black eyes glittered. "You know perfectly well that you took that rebozo from the top shelf of the closet in the hall just outside your door. Because you are working for a man who is highly respected in this community, I shall not create a scandal by reporting you to the police. But I advise you to leave town as soon as possible. Now go."

It was all so ludicrous that Cherry's anger fled and she left the room, laughing. Miss Marcia, obviously, was suffering from hallucinations, poor thing. Dr. Clem would straighten out the whole matter in the morning, and she would spend the night on the waiting-room sofa.

Upstairs in her own room Cherry began to pack. She had just finished folding her uniforms and the ones she had borrowed when she heard a stealthy sound out in the hall. For a moment Cherry was frightened. The house was so spooky, and Miss Marcia was certainly not all right mentally. Then she remembered what Coombs had said:

"The acoustics in this house are rather peculiar, miss."

Cherry shrugged and went on packing, but she couldn't help wishing that there was some way of locking her door. The stealthy—or what sounded like stealthy sounds continued, then suddenly there was a light tapping on her door. Cherry's heart leaped into her throat and she stifled a scream. Who could it be? She hadn't even seen any of the other boarders; Mrs. Briggs and Coombs were already in bed.

"Miss Ames," a voice whispered—Miss Marcia's voice.

Somehow Cherry forced herself to cross the room and open the door. "Yes, Miss Marcia?"

The woman held out the salmon-pink rebozo. "I must apologize, Miss Ames. I was mistaken. Please forgive me, Miss Ames. I am so very, very ashamed of myself." There were tears in her eyes and all of the grimness had left her face. With her lovely wavy hair flowing around her shoulders she looked so beautiful that Cherry couldn't help staring openmouthed. "Please may I come in for a moment?"

Cherry nodded, and when the door was closed, Miss Marcia continued gently, "I'm sure you won't want to stay here after my disgraceful behavior, but would you do an old woman a favor?"

"Of course," Cherry said quickly. "You don't have to apologize, Miss Marcia. Let's forget it. Anybody can make a mistake. And you're not an old woman. You're perfectly beautiful."

Miss Marcia smiled. "Let's not talk about me. What I would greatly appreciate your doing is to stay here until you find another place."

"But I don't want to leave," Cherry replied.

Miss Marcia took a deep breath and let it out slowly. "Then you have forgiven me. You are a very charitable person, my dear, and I can understand why you chose nursing for your profession. I hope you will do me the honor of having tea with me soon. Now, good night, and thank you."

After she had gone, Cherry unpacked, thinking, "I don't understand any of it, but one thing I'm sure of is that Miss Marcia is not insane and neither is she a sour old maid. Underneath her mask she's sweet and affectionate. I wonder why she wears that mask. Something must have happened to make her so bitter—something heartbreaking."

Cherry got up earlier than usual the next morning to telephone No. 9 before the girls left for work. The Manor did not boast a public phone, so she stopped off at a drugstore on her way to Dr. Clem's.

"I won't be in tomorrow," she told Gwen who answered the phone, "but I'll mail the uniforms back this morning. You should get them on Monday."

Gwen groaned. "Don't tell me why you're not going to honor us with your presence. I can guess. You're involved in another mystery—or another romance, or both."

Cherry laughed. "Well, he is very attractive and I like him a lot."

"Who?"

"Wouldn't you like to know?" Cherry teased. "How do you like your new case?"

"Don't be evasive," Gwen said firmly. *"Who?"*

"See you next Sunday," Cherry said sweetly, and hung up.

She had breakfast at the drugstore counter and went on to the post office. It was a bright sunny morning and she hummed to herself as she strolled along Main Street. "I do like Harry a lot and I want him to get elected. Lex will be furious, but I'm going to break that date."

When she got to the office she called the Answering Service and then the hospital. Lex spluttered with rage, but she placated him with:

"It's really important, Lex. I can't explain over the phone, but if you take me sightseeing tomorrow I think I can make you understand."

"Oh, all right," he growled. "Let's have breakfast together and make a day of it. Pick you up at nine."

Cherry turned on the sterilizer and sorted the mail, then she changed into uniform. By nine o'clock she had tidied the rooms, developed an X-ray which the doctor had taken the evening before, and completed a urinalysis.

"I'm glad I came in early," she reflected happily. "Now maybe I can leave earlier. I've just got a feeling that we'll find a clue in those old copies of the *Bugle* today or tonight."

Patients began to arrive then and Cherry discovered that Saturday was the busiest day of all. By eleven there was standing room only, even Cherry's desk chair and the two lab stools were being used. The phone seemed to ring incessantly and never before had Dr. Clem required her assistance in the treatment room so frequently. All kinds of shots were given, dressings were changed, hemoglobin tests were made, weights and heights were charted, temperatures were taken, prescriptions were filled out, diets were typed, rooms were reserved at the hospital, surgeons were called in reference to fractures which showed up in X-rays, and to add to the confusion a great many patients interrupted Cherry, as she dashed between the rooms, asking her how much longer they would have to wait.

Cherry moved blithely through it all; this was her chosen work and she loved it. And Dr. Clem was so calm, so good-natured, it was a real pleasure to work for him. Even the patients who grew restless were pleasant, although there were the usual arguments about the coming election.

When the noon whistle blew, there were two men and the mayor's secretary in the waiting room. Shortly after that, Harry arrived and Cherry beckoned him into the lab. "I won't be able to leave until two," she told him. "I just phoned to have a sandwich and a chocolate malted sent in. Why don't you eat and go on to the warehouse? I'll meet you there as soon as I can."

"Okay," he said, "but first I've got to tell you the good news. I spent the whole morning there and I think I've come across something which may be a clue. When he ran for supervisor, it was not by any means a landslide election. Carson also ran and darned near—"

"Sh-h," Cherry cautioned. "His secretary's out there. She might be able to hear you."

"So what?" He shrugged his broad shoulders. "I don't care if His Honor does know that I'm trying to find something shady in his past. If he's innocent, it won't faze him; if he's guilty, all the better. Nothing would make me happier than to flush that bird out of his cover." He went out through the side door.

The time clock rang and Cherry dashed into the darkroom to take the X-ray from the tank and put it on the rack to dry. When she returned to her desk she glanced at Miss Lila Jones who had previously been very restless, but who was now completely absorbed in yesterday's *Sun*.

"M-m-m," said Cherry to herself. "She could have heard what Harry said and probably did. Oh, why must that young man be so impulsive?"

It was not quite two when Cherry left the office and locked the door. Too late she realized that she had been silly not to ask Harry to come back for her. The dock was ten long blocks away, most of them downhill, fortunately, but the sidewalks were paved with rough cobblestones. She walked slowly toward the Post Road, thinking that surely Harry would remember that she didn't have a car and come back for her.

Then a big maroon sedan slowed to a stop beside her and the mayor stuck his head out of the window. "Hello, Miss Ames. Can I give you a lift anywhere?"

Overwhelmed by gratitude, Cherry threw caution to the winds and climbed in beside him. "This is very kind of you, Mr. Mayor. I didn't relish tottering over cobblestones in these high heels. Would you mind awfully driving me down to the wharf?"

"The wharf?" he repeated, elevating his bushy white eyebrows.

"That's right," Cherry replied, already regretting, for more reasons than one, that she had accepted his invitation. Although there was heavy traffic on the Post Road, he was driving so fast and so close to the car in front of him that she braced herself instinctively. They were nearing the tenement district now and she knew that because it was Saturday the narrow streets would be crowded with boys and girls. So she added quickly:

"I realize that you're in a hurry, sir. Just let me off at the next corner."

"Certainly not," he said affably. "I'm never in too much of a hurry to do a favor for a pretty girl." He turned off into Tommy's street which looked more like a playground. Mentally Cherry pushed the brake to the floor, but thank goodness the mayor inched along, tapping his horn constantly.

"The wharf," he said again. "You'll forgive my curiosity, but since the pleasure boats are all in dry dock at this time of the year, and since there are no dwellings in that area, I can't help wondering—"

He left the sentence unfinished. Cherry hastily collected her thoughts. There was very little doubt in her mind that Lila Jones had overheard what Harry had said in the lab at noon. Undoubtedly she had repeated it to her boss. That explained why he had appeared at two o'clock and offered her a lift. If she answered his implied question, he might well put two and two together and come to the conclusion that they were searching the old *Bugle* files for "something shady in his past." *If* he happened to know that the binders were in storage in the warehouse. Then, if there *was* something shady in his past, what would he do?

One of two things, Cherry decided. He would try

to prevent them from continuing their search, or he would try to get there first and destroy the clues. Either way, there was nothing she could do now. If she refused to answer his question, he would simply remain down at the dock until she entered the warehouse. There was no other place she logically could go. He broke into her thoughts suddenly:

"Ah! I see Mr. Jenner's car is parked beside the warehouse. Is that your destination, Miss Ames?"

"Yes, Mr. Mayor," she said. "And thank you very much for the lift."

He stopped so close to the old convertible that there was only a hairbreadth between the two bumpers. "A strange place for a date." His voice was so cold that Cherry's spine tingled.

She climbed out and forced herself to smile as she thanked him again and waved good-by. But as she crunched across the gravel to the door she could feel his eyes boring into her back and she was glad to get inside, dark and gloomy as it was.

The superintendent was tilted back in a chair near the entrance, but he let himself down with a bang when she came in. Without standing up or removing the cigar from the side of his mouth, he asked, "You Miss Ames?"

"That's right," Cherry said. "Mr. Jenner is expecting me."

He waved one hand apathetically. "Okay. Sign the book and go on up."

There was just enough light seeping through the

dusty, cobwebby windows so that Cherry could grope her way up the stairs.

Harry greeted her at the top. "Hi. Thought I heard a car. Hurry, hurry. Think I've got something hot."

"You did hear a car," Cherry said exasperatedly. "The mayor's car. I haven't got one, in case you've forgotten, and when he offered to give me a lift, I stupidly accepted."

"Oh, my gosh!" Harry exploded. "I was so excited about my clue I forgot that you'd have to walk. So His Honor drove you down here? Well, well, how sweet of the dear old boy. I'm surprised your hair hasn't turned as white as his. Nerve-racking, driving with him, isn't it?"

"Oh, Harry," Cherry moaned, "don't you realize that now, what with what Lila Jones overheard at Dr. Clem's, he may prevent us from ever discovering anything worth while?"

He stared at her thoughtfully. "I see what you mean. He can get a permit from the *Sun* as easily as we did, and if there is anything damaging in these old *Bugles*, he'll snatch it out of the binders pronto."

"That's what I'm afraid of," Cherry said unhappily. "So the answer is that we've got to find whatever it is, if any, before we leave here. Oh," she interrupted herself as they entered the storeroom, "how smart of you!"

Harry had hung a large lantern-type flashlight from a nail in the rafters and had brought up the seat cushions from his car. As they sat down, side by side, he

Harry said excitedly, "Read that news item first."

pointed to one of the open binders on the floor. "Read that news item first."

MARCIA CHARLTON
SERIOUSLY INJURED
IN AUTO ACCIDENT

Cherry read out loud. "But what's that got to do with the mayor?" she asked.

"Read on," he commanded.

Cherry obeyed and immediately became so absorbed that she was carried back twenty-five years ago, almost to the day, when two cars nearly collided on Bullethole Road. One of the drivers, a beautiful young ballet dancer, was on her way to New York City to make her Broadway debut, and because she started late, she took the short cut and was driving so fast that she lost control of the car and went over the embankment. The driver of the other car, which she almost crashed into, was Councilman Cyrus R. Hillman. He immediately stopped and rushed down the ravine to adminster first aid to the victim, while Mr. Turner Huland, who occupied the only house on Bullethole Road, telephoned for an ambulance. The account closed with:

"Miss Charlton is still unconscious and on the hospital's critical list. Mr. Huland, who witnessed the accident from the front porch of his home, stated that she must have been driving at the rate of eighty miles an hour, and that if Mr. Hillman had not been driving slowly, there would have been a head-on collision. Dr. Josephson stated that the councilman's prompt first-aid treatment undoubtedly saved the dancer's life. Mr. Hillman's only comment was, 'Poor little girl! I'm glad I happened to be there at the time.' "

Cherry sniffed. "I don't believe a word of it. If anyone was driving too fast, it was Cyrus R. Hillman."

"That's exactly what I think," Harry cried exultantly. "I'll bet he forced her off the road. But look at this picture which was published two weeks later. Miss Marcia has regained consciousness and is off the critical list. The photo shows her parents publicly thanking Councilman Hillman for saving their daughter's life. If he lied, why did Miss Marcia let him get by with it?"

"I think I can answer that," Cherry said slowly. "If she was unconscious for so long, she probably had a skull fracture and might well have been suffering from temporary amnesia when that picture was taken. Oh, don't you see, Harry? By the time she was completely rational and able to speak coherently, nobody would pay any attention to her. Cy Hillman was a hero and she probably was thought of as a flighty young ballet dancer. Furthermore, it all could have happened so quickly that she was confused. Lots of people who are seriously injured in an accident are so shocked that they refuse to think about it, let alone discuss it."

"I can understand that," he said. "But how about that witness, Mr. Huland?"

Cherry shook her head. "That I can't answer—unless, unless he was bribed."

"You've got it!" Harry yelled. "The accident happened a few days before election. If Cy Hillman was driving too fast and caused the accident, his political career would have ended then and there. So he had to bribe the only witness. But," he finished forlornly, "we have no proof."

"We'll get it," Cherry said determinedly. "Is Huland still living in town, Harry?"

"I never heard of him," he replied, "except that the shack on Bullethole Road which Mr. Bostwick bought last summer was always called the Huland place. And I have a vague recollection that the old one-story building which was torn down to make room for the new *Sun* building used to be Huland's Hardware Store. I may have known the guy when I was a kid, but I don't remember him."

"M-m-m," said Cherry. "If we could find something in the *Bugle*, like a bankruptcy notice, which would show that Mr. Huland was badly in need of money, we'd be a lot warmer. Or maybe the place was sold for back taxes or perhaps the mortgage was foreclosed. That kind of thing."

"If anything like that happened," Harry told her, "I should be able to find it in the records at Town Hall, but not until Monday morning."

"We can't wait," Cherry said. "Let's start with the accident and go back a few months, and this time let's watch out for the name Huland." She wrote down the date of the accident on one of the memo pads Harry had brought along and turned back to the first page in the binder. Harry took another binder from the shelf and they worked in silence for a while. Then, on one

of the society pages, Cherry saw a headline which made
her jump:

Miss Marcia Charlton
Engaged to Wed
Dr. Clemuel Brown

And in the column beside it was a picture of a beau
tiful young woman, smiling radiantly into the camera.

~~~~~~~~~~~~~~~~~~~~~~~~~~~~~~~~~~~~~~

CHAPTER XIV

An Interrupted Search

"WELL, I'LL BE A MONKEY'S UNCLE!" HARRY EXPLODED. "I always thought they hated each other."

"What a tragedy," Cherry murmured. "The engagement was announced just two weeks before the accident. That explains a lot of things."

"What for instance?"

"Why she behaves like a sour old maid, for one," Cherry replied. "Don't you see, Harry? She was seriously injured in that accident. That's why she broke the engagement. Operations and treatments are awfully expensive. Dr. Clem was a young struggling doctor in those days. She loved him too much to let him—" She left the sentence unfinished.

"I see what you mean," Harry said after a moment. "But I just can't understand Dr. Clem. Why did he let her break the engagement? He's the kind of man who would marry the woman he loved no matter what happened to her."

"I agree," Cherry said. "But it takes two people to make a marriage. Poor Miss Marcia! No wonder she's so bitter. Not only did she have to give up the man she loved, but her career as a ballet dancer ended on the eve of her Broadway debut. And I think I know now why, eventually, she had to take in boarders. Even though her parents apparently had a lot of money at the time of the accident, they probably spent most of it on operations and treatments."

"That could be," Harry admitted. "But I still don't see why she and Dr. Clem didn't get married after her leg was practically cured. Neither one of them married anybody else, so—"

"It probably was too late then," Cherry broke in. "She must have said or done something pretty drastic in the beginning, in order to convince him that she would never marry him. You wouldn't guess it from that mask she wears, but she's got a quick, fiery temper." She told him about the scene she had had the night before with her landlady.

Harry was dumfounded. "Do you mean she actually ordered you out of the house at that time of night?"

"I don't blame her now," Cherry said. "I've been thinking about that rebozo. I'll bet Dr. Clem bought one from Maria that was exactly like mine and sent it to Miss Marcia for Christmas. Just because she won't let him come into her home doesn't mean he can't send her anonymous presents—if he still loves her. And if she still loves him she'd treasure those presents more than anything else in the world. No wonder she was so furious when she thought I'd stolen one of them."

"I think you're letting your imagination run away with you," Harry said bluntly. "Let's get back to work."

"All right." Meekly Cherry began scanning the newspapers again, but they found nothing of interest. At seven o'clock Harry said disgruntledly:

"Let's knock off for an hour and have a decent dinner for a change."

"I'm starving," Cherry agreed, "and even when I close my eyes I can still see print."

They signed out and drove along the river road to an attractive inn named the Phantom Ship. When they had given the cheerful colored waiter their order, Cherry asked:

"Why is this place called the Phantom Ship?"

"Because of the legend," Harry explained. "This part of the Hudson is called the Tappan Zee, and during the Revolution it was invested by British men-of-war from which raiding parties were sent ashore in rowboats to forage for food. The story goes that one of the ships was sunk but its ghost still remains, and to this day you'll meet river people who will swear that they have glimpsed her topsails glittering in the moonbeams. Another legend is that she is the ghost of Henry Hudson's *Half Moon*. There are plenty of people who claim to have seen her burst from a thundercloud and that's why she's also called the Storm Ship."

Cherry shivered delightedly. "Tell me some more of the legends. Ichabod Crane and Rip Van Winkle are two of my favorite characters."

"When we visit West Point," Harry said, "we'll continue on up to the Catskills and we'll climb a winding path to the very rock where Rip was supposed to have slept for twenty years. I couldn't begin to tell you all of the legends now; there are so many of them. Besides the Headless Horseman, there are all sorts of ghosts and hobgoblins and witches who are supposed to inhabit this region. Dobbs Ferry, for instance, is a large town farther down the river on this side. It was named after Jeremiah Dobb who used to ferry folks across to the west shore. I've met plenty of people who claim to have heard his oars at midnight. Others have seen his ghost in his ancient dugout, especially on Halloween, which, by the way, is next Wednesday."

"Tommy told me about the Dobb ghost the other day—" Cherry began, but Harry interrupted:

"Speaking of Tommy, Thursday is the first of November. I don't like the idea of his biking out to Bullethole Road alone at dusk, do you? If the mayor suspects he noticed those meetings with the New York taxi driver there might be another, quote, accident, quote, closed."

"Tommy won't be biking anywhere next week," Cherry said. "He's in bed with hot poultices on that knee. His cousin Mike O'Brien is handling the route for him. Anyway, aren't we going to be among those present next Thursday at six o'clock?"

"Why, yes," Harry said with a grin. "I think it would be a good idea for us to cruise casually along Bullethole Road around that time. I can't wait to see who comes up from New York on the first of every month to meet the mayor. And I'd like to know why; also why they meet at such an isolated spot."

"I don't think that taxi has a passenger," Cherry said. "Remember, Tommy said that only the driver is in it when it goes back. Since we read about Miss Marcia's accident, I've been thinking that the mayor has a rendezvous every month with the taxi driver who may well be Mr. Turner Huland!"

Harry dropped his fork with a clatter. "Blackmail?"

"It follows, doesn't it?" Cherry asked. "A man who would accept a bribe wouldn't hesitate to try a little extortion in order to get more money. Especially when the man he's blackmailing is the mayor."

"You're a genius," Harry said. "It also explains why the mayor had to get complete control of some of the town's funds. And why we have substandard tenements and no playgrounds. And why getting re-elected every term is a matter of life or death to him. The minute he loses office he's ruined."

"Oh, I think the blackmailing would stop then," Cherry argued. "Maybe it would never have started if he hadn't risen to such a high position. After all, you can't get blood from a stone."

Harry signaled the waiter and paid the check. "There's no sense in our sitting around theorizing. We've got to get some proof."

It was pitch dark when they parked beside the warehouse. Harry gave Cherry a torch and carried the lantern-type flashlight himself. Tim O'Brien let them in, grumbling, "What goes on? Why can't people stay home nights? Don't forget to sign the book."

"Yes, sir," said Harry with the pencil poised over the page. Then he groaned, "Oh, *no*. Look, Cherry. We're too late."

Cherry peered over his shoulder and saw to her dismay that two lines had been filled in after they signed out:

> *Cyrus R. Hillman, Mayor* . . . 7:10 P.M. *In*
> *Cyrus R. Hillman, Mayor* . . . 8:15 P.M. *Out*

Harry whirled on the old night watchman. "Did the mayor have a permit to enter the *Sun's* storeroom?"

"Don't let anybody in without a permit," Tim O'Brien replied. "Not even the mayor himself. You two going to sign the book or not? I can't stand around here all night. I've got work to do, and I'm tired. Night's only just begun and I'm dog-tired already."

"You wouldn't be so tired, Mr. O'Brien," Cherry said gently, "if you'd take those vitamin capsules Dr. Clem gave you."

He glowered at her. "Can't swallow 'em. It's a family failing. None of us can swallow pills."

"Tommy can," Cherry pointed out, "and he's your nephew."

He snorted. "Don't let him fool you. He's ashamed to admit it, that's all."

Cherry gasped. "Do you mean Tommy hasn't been taking the antibiotic Dr. Clem gave him?"

The old man shrugged. "Don't know what you call

it, but I was sitting right there in the kitchen when he tossed that bottle in the trash can."

Cherry grabbed Harry's arm. "This is awful. Please drive me to the office right away. Tommy's knee might get badly infected. What a silly boy he was not to tell me he couldn't swallow capsules! Tetracyn comes in a chocolate-flavored liquid form and there are some samples of it in the lab. I want to bring a bottle to Tommy right away."

"Okay," Harry said. "There's no sense in hanging around here any longer. You can count on it that there's nothing in the *Bugle* files now which might be damaging to His Honor's character."

"That doesn't bother me," Cherry said as they started up the hill toward the Post Road. "Even if we put dozens of twos and twos together to make fours, we still wouldn't have had any real proof."

"True," he admitted, "but enough facts for me to base questions on when I next write a letter to the *Sun*. For instance, if we could have discovered that Mr. Huland was badly in need of money and suddenly, *unaccountably*, obtained a large sum around the time of Miss Marcia's accident."

"Mrs. Nellie Carson might be able to tell us things like that," Cherry suggested. "She seems to like me and she certainly despises Mr. Hillman. Since her husband was in politics for so many years she might well have a scrapbook. Let's call on her this evening after I bring a bottle of Tetracyn to Tommy." She sighed. "I could spank that boy. Dr. Clem gave him a shot of penicillin on Tuesday when he sutured the wound, but yesterday, when he removed the sutures, he saw that an abscess was forming, so he prescribed two hundred milligrams of Tetracyn four times daily. I gave Tommy a sample bottle of capsules, not knowing that he couldn't swallow them. Now I feel so worried and guilty. I should have asked him—"

"It wasn't your fault," Harry interrupted. "Dr. Clem should have told you, instead of taking for granted that you knew. You can't be expected to pick up all of the patients' idiosyncrasies in one short week."

"He's so used to Lola," Cherry said thoughtfully. "Nobody could ever really take her place. I hope she gets married and goes back to work for him."

"Well, I don't," Harry said firmly. "If she goes back to him, you'll leave town. That can't happen." He stopped in front of the doctor's house and Cherry raced into the lab and came right out again. As they drove back toward the tenement district, she said:

"I've thought of a plan which would give us something which you could write about to the *Sun* if we can't get any information from Mrs. Carson."

"I've thought of a wonderful plan myself," he said smugly. "Lola can go back to work for Dr. Clem. Then when I'm mayor you'll be my secretary."

Cherry giggled. "You should see my shorthand—a thing of my own invention."

"I'll get a dictaphone."

"I type at a snail's pace."

He grinned at her sidewise. "I'll hire a typist."

"You seem awfully sure of being elected," Cherry teased.

"I am," he retorted and sobered. "If we can ever get started, the whole thing would snowball very fast. I mean, if the old-timers in this town even suspected that Cy Hillman caused that accident twenty-five years ago they'd turn on him in righteous wrath. Why don't you have tea with Miss Marcia soon, Cherry, and tell her everything we know? If you refreshed her memory, she might make some sort of a statement which the *Sun* would publish."

"We don't know anything," Cherry argued. "How can I refresh her memory with theories? But if I could tell her for sure that Cy Hillman has a clandestine meeting on the first of every month with Turner Huland, I think that would start *her* to thinking back until she arrived at the same conclusion that we did—that the witness was bribed."

Harry groaned. "How we can we prove that? We don't even know what Huland looks like, and even if we did, he's bound to have changed a lot in the last quarter of a century. So getting a glimpse of that taxi driver isn't going to prove anything."

"I'm not interested in getting a glimpse of his face," Cherry said. "What I'm interested in is seeing the hack license which is always attached to the back of the front seat. If the name on the license is Turner Huland, then we'll be able to start that snowball rolling!"

CHAPTER XV

More Clues

"IT'S AN ILL WIND THAT BLOWS NO GOOD," HARRY SAID as he parked near Tommy's home. "Mrs. Regan will have to let you into their apartment now, so you'll have a chance to see what this tenement is really like inside." He helped her climb out to the cobblestoned sidewalk. "Go in through the main entrance instead of via the cellar steps. I feel sure one glance at the hall will convince you that not a penny has been spent on the interior of the building since the town took it over six or seven years ago. The other tenements are, believe it or not, in far worse shape because they have been town-owned for many more years."

Cherry did as Harry suggested and was even more shocked than he had predicted. The sagging floor in the unlighted hall was dangerously pitted with holes, strips of plaster and a broken electrical fixture dangled precariously from the ceiling, and the staircase was full of gaps caused by missing steps. When her eyes grew accustomed to the semidarkness, Cherry groped her way along the rough, unpainted walls until she found a door on which was thumbtacked a neat card bearing the printed word: SUPER.

Mrs. Regan came up from the cellar in answer to her knock, and five minutes later Cherry was sitting on the foot of Tommy's narrow cot. "I'm surprised at you," she scolded him gently. "Lots of people have trouble swallowing large capsules. That's nothing to be ashamed of."

He grinned up at her sheepishly. "That chocolate stuff tasted good. Is my knee getting better, Miss Cherry, or will I get a great big boil? I've just got to get back to work."

"Your knee is doing fine," Cherry said cheerfully. She turned to his worn little mother. "Is he eating well, Mrs. Regan? Dr. Clem thinks that he wouldn't have developed that abscess if he weren't so run-down and thin."

Tommy's eight-year-old sister spoke up, "None of us gets enough to eat. Mr. Hillman is s'posed to give Mommy lots more money than he does for running the furnace and everything, but just because she's not a man—"

"Sh-h, Dottie," Mrs. Regan silenced her. "Mr. Hillman is very good to let us live here without paying any rent."

Cherry glanced around the damp, crowded room. "Well, I don't think he's good to you at all," she said exasperatedly. "I understand why you don't dare complain, but I can't understand the other tenants."

"They don't dare complain either, Miss Cherry," the frail little woman replied. "If the building is torn down, where would they go? There's no place else where the rent is so cheap."

"The building wouldn't have to be torn down," Cherry said. "All it needs is a few thousand dollars spent on repairs and improvements. Besides, the rent isn't cheap. Your sister-in-law, Mrs. O'Brien, told me yesterday in Dr. Clem's office that they pay fifty dollars a month for three wretched little rooms on the top floor. It's outrageous!"

"When we owned the building," Mrs. O'Brien said softly, "we kept it real nice. Thomas had a night job with the railroad, but he didn't spend his days sleeping. He was always painting or putting in new pipes and things like that."

"I'm sure he did." Cherry smiled and said good-by. When she joined Harry in the car outside she told him, "It makes my blood boil. I'm going to report that building to the health and the fire commissioners."

"Go ahead," he said, "but you won't get anywhere. The only way you can get any action is for the town board to duly appoint an official for the sole purpose of inspecting unsafe dwellings and making a report of same to the board. But the board won't appoint anybody, because they take the mayor's word for it that these buildings do not violate any fire or health laws.

And you can't blame the board for that attitude, in view of the fact that he has been granted enormous sums for the very purpose of making them safe and secure."

"I guess only a lawyer can understand it," Cherry said with a sigh. "Let's go see Nellie Carson. I have a feeling she is going to be on our side."

As they drove along the avenue, Harry said, "I'd like to know how you plan to get a glimpse of that hack license. My idea was to get the number on the registration plate and then check with the Bureau of Motor Vehicles in New York to find out who owns the cab."

"That won't do us any good if it happens to be one of a chain," Cherry pointed out. "This is my plan: We'll go to Bullethole Road via the parkway and stop on that side of Mr. Bostwick's house. If the road is as narrow as you say it is, and you park right smack in the middle as though you had run out of gas, the taxi will have to stop. While you're talking to the driver, asking him to give us a lift to the nearest gas station, I'll climb into the back. If he refuses to accept us as a fare, which he probably will, I'll still have time to see the name on the hack license."

"Wow!" Harry cried admiringly. "You should have been a criminal lawyer. That scheme can't miss."

"I hope not, but anyway, I'm glad you approve of it." Cherry took out her compact and powdered her nose. "Now let's hope Mrs. Carson will be able to give us some clues."

Nellie Carson, when they laid their cards on the table and told her what they suspected, was wildly enthusiastic. "Mr. Carson was always suspicious," she told them. "We both knew that Marcia Charlton was a careful driver and that Cyrus Hillman was a speed maniac. But what could we do, in view of that witness's statement? What was his name?"

"Turner Huland," Harry said. "Did you know him, Miss Nellie?"

She pursed her lips. "Not to speak to. He was always a no-good; never got through high school, always hanging around poolrooms, and they say he bet on the horses. All I really know about him is that he inherited that house and the plot of land around it from his grandfather. It used to be a hunting lodge, but Huey—that's what they called him—never kept it up. I remember now that Mr. Carson told me once that it was going to be sold for back taxes, but it wasn't. Just before Huey left town—and good riddance—he sold it to somebody or other. I can't remember now; that place has changed hands so many times. I understand a Mr. Bostwick bought it last summer. Why anybody would want to live in such a ramshackle place is beyond me!"

"Do you remember when Huey left town?" Cherry asked.

The plump woman smoothed the skirt of her red velvet hostess gown. The diamonds and sapphires on her beringed fingers flashed in the light from the flaming logs in the fireplace. "Not exactly, but it wasn't long after Cyrus Hillman became town supervisor. I remember that election very well because Mr. Carson was running against him. He would have won, too, if there hadn't been so much publicity about how Cyrus saved Marcia's life by applying a tourniquet to her leg. Marcia, you see, was the town's darling; our pride and joy. She would have been a world-famous ballet dancer, and she was as beautiful as she was graceful. It was all so tragic I can't bear to think about it." She covered her face with her hands. "We've had so many tragedies—so many. I try not to brood, but I can't help it. Clem Brown is the only person who can cheer me up."

"He and Miss Marcia were engaged, weren't they?" Cherry asked.

Mrs. Carson nodded. "They didn't announce it until he started in practice, but they were childhood sweethearts. We all feared that he would go to pieces during those awful days when she was in the hospital. Not long after she came home they quarreled. I can't for the life of me think what about. All I know is that when her parents were so dreadfully ill she wouldn't let him treat them. Of course he was a very young doctor, but still, there was no reason for ordering him never to put his foot inside her home. That dear, sweet, kind good man! I love him better than any living person. And I've never spoken to Marcia Charlton since she ordered him out of The Manor." She put her hand to her throat. "I mustn't start brooding about things that happened in the past. But what else can I do? If only I were well enough to do the things I used to do when Mr. Carson was alive."

Cherry said quietly, "I know you give a great deal to charity, Mrs. Carson, but did you ever visit the tenements down by the water front?"

"Not for the past ten years," Mrs. Carson replied. "I did a lot of that kind of work when I was a Gray Lady. But I'm too old now."

"I don't think you are," Cherry corrected her gently. "I think if you visited some of our patients and saw the conditions under which they're living you'd want to do something for them. I don't mean money, but we haven't nearly enough visiting nurses and social workers to go around. You could do things like keeping hot poultices on a boy's knee, couldn't you?"

Mrs. Carson tossed her head. "Certainly. I was not only a Gray Lady but a Nurse's Aide too. Do you really mean that there are people in this town who would find an old fool like me useful?"

Cherry laughed. "Lots of them, but you're not an old fool." She stood up and held out her hand. "I'll bring you a list of names and addresses tomorrow. Good night, Mrs. Carson."

When they were out on the street, Harry said, "Boy! You certainly killed a lot of birds with one stone that time! Nellie Carson is as good as cured of her hypochondria and a lot of poor people are going to get food and clothing they badly need."

"She's not really a hypochondriac," Cherry said firmly. "She's got a slight case of melancholia, plus a lot of utter boredom. I hope she calls on Tommy Regan tomorrow. Wouldn't it be wonderful if she got interested in him and sent him to college?"

"It could happen," Harry agreed. "That kid deserves a break. He'd sell those savings bonds the *Sun* awards him and turn the money over to his mother, but she won't let him."

"She's a wonderful person," Cherry said. "I don't know how she does all that heavy work. She's no bigger than a minute. When you get right down to it, Tim O'Brien is a wonder, too. Most people suffering from such a painful case of osteoarthritis would go on relief."

"I've always liked and admired the Regans and O'Briens," Harry told her. "Well, where to now? It's only ten o'clock and Saturday night."

"Home and to bed for me," Cherry said firmly. "I've suddenly discovered that I'm utterly exhausted."

"It's been quite a day," he agreed, "and we certainly accomplished a lot. I can't wait until you have tea with Miss Marcia and find out how she feels about our clues and theories."

"And I," Cherry returned, "can't wait until Thursday. If that taxi driver is Huey Huland, I'm willing to bet my rebozo that you'll be our next mayor, Harry."

CHAPTER XVI

~~~~~~

A Day with Lex

SUNDAY WAS ANOTHER WARM, SUNNY DAY. AS CHERRY
and Lex drove north on their way to the Franklin Del-
ano Roosevelt estate near Hyde Park, she told him what
she and Harry had discovered in the old *Bugle* files. He
listened in amazement but refused to take her seriously
when she wound up with:

"If we can prove that the taxi driver is blackmailing
the mayor, you'll vote for Harry, won't you?"

"You and your vivid imagination!" he exploded. "But
I'm sure glad you've lifted the veil over Miss Marcia's
past. Now I can understand why she seems so sour at
times. I've always felt that she was wearing sort of a
protective mask, and instead of being frozen, she's always on the verge of tears or laughter."

"She's got a quick, red-hot temper, too," Cherry began, and then decided not to tell him about the rebozo
scene.

"We're approaching Harmon," he was saying. "I guess you know it's the station where trains going north from New York change from electric engines to steam. And vice versa, of course. Now we're passing the famous Van Cortlandt Manor. Looks a lot like Miss Marcia's, doesn't it?"

Cherry nodded. "They're practically twins!"

"Olaff Stevense Van Cortlandt," Lex continued, "was the founder of the family and he arrived in America in 1638 as a soldier employed by the Dutch West India Company. His son, Stephanus, first lord of the manor, bought from Indians and early settlers more than eighty-seven thousand acres of land. The northern border, a distance that an Indian could walk in a day, is now the boundary between Westchester and Putnam counties. It extends southward along the Hudson from Anthony's Nose almost to Manhattan."

"I've been to Van Cortlandt Park in New York," Cherry said, "and I knew it was named after a famous old family, but I didn't know their land extended this far up."

"We'll go inside the manor house sometime," Lex said, "but first I want to buy you a bouquet in Rhinebeck, which is famous for its violets. We'll take in Hyde Park on our way back, have lunch, then go to the Tarrytowns—Sleepy Hollow Land."

They ate on the porch of the Half Moon Inn, an attractive place on top of a hill overlooking the river.

"I'm falling under the spell of the Hudson," Cherry said dreamily. "Having spent most of my life on the flat

Midwestern prairies, I'm constantly awed by the mountains around here."

"Well," said Lex grimly, "just so long as you don't fall under the spell of a human being. I'm still not convinced you had to break your date with me last night. Just for that, I'm not going to vote for Harry Jenner after all."

"Even if the taxi driver turns out to be Huey Huland?" Cherry asked. He nodded, grinning.

Cherry tossed her head. "Well, if you ever saw the inside of one of those tenements, you wouldn't vote for Cyrus Hillman. Why don't you go and see for yourself, Lex?"

"I will," he promised, "when I get off duty on Thursday afternoon."

"One thing I'll never understand," Cherry continued, "is why some of the doctors in Sleepyside haven't raised a fuss and reported those tenements to the health commissioner. Dr. Clem, for instance, must have been inside one of them since they were allowed to go to rack and ruin."

"Not necessarily," Lex argued. "Poor people can rarely afford house calls. They go to the clinic or to Dr. Clem, which amounts to the same thing, because he charges them so little, if any. A lot of people, like the Regans and O'Briens, are too proud to ask for charity. If they did, a visiting nurse would be sent to them as well as a social worker. Instead, they doctor themselves until they either get well or are so far gone that an ambulance has to be sent. Interns," he reminded her, "ride the ambulance. And interns don't feel it's their duty to report social conditions to the health commissioner."

Cherry sighed. "I guess you're right, but it seems to me that somebody in authority ought to have done something about those tenements a long time ago. And now that Harry has called them to the attention of the public in his letter which was published in last Sunday's *Sun*, why doesn't the town board appoint somebody to investigate?"

Lex thought for a minute. "I guess maybe *you're* right. Cy Hillman seems to have our government under his thumb. And since this is a democracy, he can't really be a good mayor. But before I form a definite opinion, I'm going to inspect those tenements myself. I know you, Cherry. You're apt to exaggerate when you're emotionally involved. And since Harry is Cy's opponent in the mayoralty race, it wouldn't be fair for me to accept as facts what may merely be his opinions."

"You're the stubbornest man in the world," Cherry said impatiently. "But I have to admire you for it. And probably there are a lot of influential people in town just like you; they have to see for themselves. Oh, I do hope Mrs. Carson keeps her promise and calls on Tommy this very morning. If she does, I'm sure she'll be up in arms when she sees that crowded, dank basement apartment."

"Nellie could do your side a lot of good," Lex agreed, "but she might also do you some harm. We in the medical profession understand her imaginary illnesses, but other people think she's just plain silly. Now, if you could get Miss Marcia and Dr. Clem on Harry's side, he'd carry the town easily."

"I'm going to work on them both," Cherry said. "Now let's do some more sightseeing."

As they drove south along the river road, Lex asked, "How much do you remember of your American history?"

Cherry bristled. "As much as you do, I'll bet. Why?"

"Well," said Lex, "first on our list is Patriots' Park on the border line between the Tarrytowns. There you'll see a statue of John Paulding. Who was he?"

"I have no idea," Cherry admitted ruefully.

"Hah," said Lex triumphantly. "He was one of three Colonial irregulars who captured Major John André. The monument in Patriots' Park commemorates the incident. Who was André?"

Cherry sighed. "It escapes me at the moment."

Lex chuckled. "André was quite a guy—charming, brave, gallant, and so forth, but he happened to be adjutant general of the British army in America during the Revolution. West Point, of course, was one of the vital strategic points, and André was carrying on negotiations with Benedict Arnold who was in command of the post. In September, 1780, the traitor sold André plans, describing our defenses in detail. On his way back to the British lines, André, disguised as a patriot, was challenged by John Paulding, David Williams, and Isaac Van Wart. They could discover nothing suspicious and were about to let him pass when Paulding decided to examine André's boots. The plans of West

Point were in one of them. André was taken to Washington's headquarters at Tappan and eventually hanged as a spy, though both armies mourned his death."

"I remember all of that now," Cherry said. "But I never could understand why a hero like Benedict Arnold became a traitor."

"He was a great man in many ways," Lex agreed. "He was one of our generals who won the important Battle of Saratoga. His left leg was wounded during the victorious charge against Burgoyne, and there is a lifelike memorial of his leg on the Saratoga Battlefield. The idea being that his left leg was the only part of him which was loyal to his country."

Lex slowed to a stop. "There's the statue of Paulding. I don't know of any monument to David Williams, but Isaac Van Wart was rewarded for the part he played in the capture of André in another, rather amusing way. The village of Dobbs Ferry, which is a few miles farther down the river, was named after him. But the name didn't stick because, obviously, Wart-on-Hudson is not too lovely a name, and by a special act of state legislature, the village became Dobbs Ferry again."

Cherry laughed, and they drove on and slowly past the old Dutch burying ground of Sleepy Hollow. "Washington Irving was buried there," Lex told her. "And this is the very place where the Headless Horseman 'tethered his horse nightly among the graves.' "

Cherry shivered. "Didn't you say that there's a replica of the Headless Horseman Bridge at the Philipse Castle Restoration?"

"That's right," Lex said. "And that's our next stop. The Old Dutch Church was erected by the Lord of Philipse Castle at the latter part of the seventeenth century. Frederick Philipse, first lord of the manor, was noted for his enormous holdings and many activities. The stone mansion and the millhouse were built on the millpond around that time. The wooden, or Beekman, addition was added in 1785. The Widow Beekman was a Van Cortlandt, and the Philipse land, as was the huge Van Cortlandt acreage, was originally purchased from the Indians. Miss Marcia's ancestors intermarried with all three families, and she owns duplicates of many of the relics you're going to see."

They spent an hour at the Restoration and then went on to visit Washington Irving's home. Sunnyside was, Cherry discovered as they approached the many-gabled house, exactly as Irving himself had described it: "as full of angles and corners as an old cocked hat." As they wandered, enchanted, through the lovely rooms, she said to Lex:

"No wonder Thackeray called Irving 'a delightful example of complete gentlemanhood.'"

Lex nodded. "And you know, in spite of the way she acts sometimes, I've always thought of Miss Marcia as a perfect example of complete gentle*lady*hood. Now that you've uncovered the tragedy in her past I can understand why she is so bitter."

"It's her pride which caused the real tragedy," Cherry said thoughtfully. "Right after the accident she must have said or done something cruel to drive Dr. Clem away from her—to convince him that she would never marry him. Later, she probably regretted it, but it was too late then. He has his pride, too."

"You mean," Lex asked, "that he can never forgive her for whatever she did?"

"No," Cherry said thoughtfully. "I honestly think that if we could ever get those two together they'd fall into each other's arms."

"What makes you think so?" Lex glanced at her sharply.

"The rebozo," Cherry said mysteriously. "I think I've solved the mystery of the missing rebozo."

"Stop talking jargon," Lex commanded as he stopped in front of The Manor. "You sound as though you were suffering from a slight case of sightseeing exhaustion. You'd better not see another sight until our dinner date at seven thirty on Thursday."

Cherry waved good-by to him from the front steps, thinking, "I hope I see a sight on Thursday at six o'clock. That taxi driver just *has* to be Huey Huland!"

CHAPTER XVII

The Rendezvous

THE FIRST CHANCE CHERRY GOT ON MONDAY SHE ASKED Dr. Clem:

"Have you ever been in the Regans' apartment, sir?"

He thought for a moment. "Not since Dottie was a baby. They're a pretty healthy crew and if anything's wrong they come to see me. Mostly it's for shots or for treatment of minor injuries. The older kids had the childhood diseases before Dottie was born and she seems to be immune so far."

"Then you don't know, Dr. Clem, that they're living in three basement rooms?" Cherry sat in the chair beside his desk. When he shook his head in bewilderment, she went on, "I didn't think you did. And I'll bet you haven't been in the O'Briens' flat for the past six or seven years, either."

"I don't think I have," he admitted. "Should I?"

"I think so," Cherry said, and explained.

He stared at her in amazement. "Things can't be as bad as that. The men in our government are honest and sincerely have the interests of the town at heart."

"I don't think the mayor has," Cherry objected. "I think he is ruthlessly selfish. For example, he was the cause of Tommy's bike accident, and he didn't even stop to find out if the boy was badly hurt. He was also the cause of Harry's accident; for the same reason, driving too fast. In my opinion, people who drive too fast are ruthlessly selfish."

"True," Dr. Clem conceded. "But can you prove that he did cause those accidents?"

"No," Cherry replied, "and I can't prove that he caused another, much more serious accident, but I'm going to try to get the proof—or, at least, a combination of truths which will indicate that it was he—" she suddenly decided to take the plunge "that it was he, not Miss Marcia Charlton, who was driving too fast on Bullethole Road that evening twenty-five years ago."

Dr. Clem jumped. Then, resting his elbows on the desk, he buried his face in his hands. "Cherry, Cherry," she heard him murmur, "you don't know what you're saying. Don't bring up the dead past. You'll only reopen healed wounds."

"You still love her, don't you, Dr. Clem?" Cherry asked softly.

He uncovered his face. "Of course I love her—she's the only woman I ever could love. But she hates me. I don't know why; I don't know why. At first I attributed her attitude to the shock of the accident; the skull fracture; the prognosis that she would never dance again. But even after she came home from the hospital she refused to see me. Then her parents took her abroad for an operation by a famous surgeon. She never answered my letters, and when she came back, months later, she still refused to see me." He closed his eyes, and Cherry knew that he was living in the past. "The unkindest cut of all was when her parents were struck down during an influenza epidemic. I didn't call with the idea of taking the case, but because they were dear, dear friends of mine; a second set of parents, you might say. But she refused to let me into the house and ordered me never to come back." His face was drawn with pain. "Why?"

Cherry tried to swallow the lump in her throat. "Because she loves you, Dr. Clem. I can understand her attitude, and I know she still loves you. Won't you, please, try to see her one more time?"

He wiped his eyes with his handkerchief. "Not unless she sends for me. You're wrong when you say she loves me. She hates the very sight of me. And I don't know why. I don't know why." He stood up suddenly. "It's almost one and I'm due at the Day Nursery. When I leave there, I'll have a bit to eat and try to go on to the Regans for a look at Tommy's knee."

Cherry watched him leave, thinking, "If only I could get those two together!" Then she notified the Answering Service that she was going out for lunch and ran across the street for a sandwich and a cup of coffee. Harry was at the counter, starting on a piece of pie.

"I've actually got a rich client," he told her gleefully.

"And it's all due to you. Nellie Carson is going to sue the town and wants me to represent her."

Cherry stared at him. "How can she sue the town?"

"For many reasons," he replied. "It so happens that she owns property which adjoins the tenement district and she feels that they constitute fire hazards which endanger the buildings on her property."

"Oh," Cherry broke in, "then she must have called on Tommy yesterday!"

"She called on everybody on your list," he said. "When that gal gets going, there's no stopping her. She's in a rage about the whole thing. Started right out by turning her ankle when she got out of her limousine and she's going to sue the town because the street isn't properly paved. Also, because it's too narrow. As a property owner she knows about a lot of the town laws and specifications which I'm not familiar with, but with which I am rapidly becoming familiar. Wow! If we've really got a case and I can work up a brief in time, her suit will knock our beloved mayor's campaign into a cocked hat."

"Maybe," Cherry said dubiously. "It might help our side some, but Lex says that a lot of people think that Nellie is just plain silly. If nobody takes her lawsuit seriously—"

"They will," Harry interrupted emphatically. "The only hitch is that I may not be able to finish my brief and file a complaint before Election Day. So if you don't see me until our Thursday date, you'll understand why."

"That suits me fine," Cherry said cheerfully. "I'm way behind on my own work."

It was true, and when she returned to the office after lunch she was kept busy until the evening office hours began. She hadn't really been neglecting things, but she was not as far ahead as she would have liked. There were dressings to be made, solutions to be changed, supplies to be checked, and filing to be done. She filled Dr. Clem's fountain pen, saw that he was well supplied with stationery and blank history cards, then she watered the flowers and plants and gave them all vitamins. After that, she sorted the magazines and discarded the old and tattered ones. She gathered up the medical journals and arranged them in chronological order in the doctor's bookcase with his textbooks.

Then she settled down to bring her bookkeeping up to date. "Thursday is the first," she reflected a bit nervously, "and that's when I'll start sending out statements. I really shouldn't take the afternoon off, but if I work late Wednesday night, maybe I'll be able to mail all of the statements on Thursday morning."

This turned out to be true with a few exceptions. On Thursday morning Dr. Clem gave Cherry a list of the house calls he had made on Wednesday night, so she made out statements including those fees after office hours. To save time, Cherry had her lunch sent in that day and ate it in the lab after the last patient left.

Mrs. Regan came in to do the cleaning at two and Cherry said, "Hope I won't be in your way. How's Tommy's knee? Dr. Clem has been trying to find time to drop in and see him, but he's been terribly busy night and day."

"I know," the frail little woman replied as she tied a bandanna around her curly brown hair. "And there's no need for him to see Tommy. That chocolate liquid you gave him worked like magic. That boil isn't coming to a head. It's fading away."

"Good. If Dr. Clem doesn't get a chance to see him today or this evening, I'll drop in on him tomorrow around three. I hear that he and Mrs. Carson are crazy about each other."

"That they are," Tommy's mother agreed. "She's a lovely lady. Knows a lot about nursing too." She plugged in the vacuum cord and Cherry went back to her desk work. When she had sealed and stamped all of the envelopes, she arranged them in alphabetical order and typed out a list of the names under the heading *Bills Mailed November 1st*. Then she tidied her desk, changed from uniform into her red woolen suit, and brought the statements to the post office. It was five thirty when she returned to Dr. Clem's and found Harry waiting for her.

"Nervous?" he asked with a grin as they climbed into his jalopy which he had parked at the side entrance.

"Certainly not," Cherry said firmly. "I checked those figures three times."

He chuckled. "We're obviously talking on different subjects. I'm discussing our business on Bullethole Road."

"Oh," Cherry said. "What's there to be nervous

about? I'm only afraid we may be disappointed. Suppose there isn't a rendezvous, and even if there is, the taxi driver may not be Huey Huland."

He drove up a ramp to the broad four-lane parkway and slowly headed north. The sun had disappeared behind the mountaintops and dusk was settling over the flaming sky. It was much colder now than it had been at sunset and Cherry wished she had worn a topcoat. "Or maybe," she reflected, "my hands and feet are cold because I really am nervous." Aloud she asked: "How's the brief progressing?"

"Slowly but surely," he told her. "We've got a case all right. Even if I can't file a complaint in time, I'm going to prepare a statement for Nellie to release to the *Sun*. I just want to be sure that there's nothing libelous in it." He left the parkway, drove under a bridge, and stopped at the entrance to a road which was almost completely hidden by the red-and-gold leaves of the maple trees. "Here we are," he began, and was immediately interrupted by the tooting of a horn.

They both turned and jumped. Right behind them was a New York taxi! Harry hastily backed away from the entrance and the cab shot past them. "Well," he exploded, "we couldn't have timed it better!"

"Did you get a glimpse of the driver?" Cherry asked. "I didn't. You were in my way."

He shook his head. "The visor of his cap was pulled way down over his face. That in itself is suspicious. I'm beginning to feel that we're not going to be disappointed, Cherry."

Harry waited a few minutes, then drove into the road and bumped slowly along it until they caught sight of the shack on the left. On the right was a steep embankment that sloped sharply down to a gully which was now a bed of autumn leaves. Cherry shivered, thinking about that evening twenty-five years ago.

"I don't see how anybody could drive fast on this road," she said. "Why, it's nothing but ruts."

He turned off the ignition. "Don't forget that it's in much worse shape than it was twenty-five years ago." They climbed out and Cherry began to pace up and down in front of the bumper while Harry lifted the hood and peered at the motor, assuming an attitude of thorough disgust.

"Now I am nervous," Cherry admitted. "If the case comes to court and we're witnesses, we really should have seen the meeting between the two men."

"The accident case will never come to court," Harry assured her. "On account of the statute of limitations. All we can do is supply the public with enough facts so they can put two and two together and come to the conclusion that Cy bribed Huey, and that Huey is now blackmailing Cy."

They both tensed as they heard a car coming from the other direction. In a moment the taxi rounded the bend below the shack and came bumping toward them. When it was close enough, they began to wave and shout:

"Taxi! Taxi!"

For a moment it looked as though the driver were not

going to stop, but when he realized that he couldn't squeeze by, he did. He stuck his head out of the window and yelled:

"Get that heap out of my way. I'm in a hurry."

They hurried toward him, and when Cherry reached for the door handle, he yelped:

"Get outta there! I ain't takin' no fares. Can't you see my flag's down?"

"We're out of gas," Harry panted.

Cherry turned the handle.

"Won't you give us a lift to the nearest gas station?" Harry asked.

"No, I won't!"

Cherry leaned inside as far as she could.

"You get away from there," he shouted, racing the motor. "I'm gonna back up and turn around. If you get hurt, it's not my fault! I warned you."

Cherry jumped clear just in time. He backed with a grinding of gears, jerked forward, backed again, and drove off.

"What a charming fellow," Harry said, scribbling on a note pad. "Well, we've got his registration number, anyway."

"He's Huey Huland all right," Cherry said. "The light goes on when the door opens and I got a good look at his hack license. It belongs to no other than Turner Huland, and the photograph on the license proves that he was driving the cab!"

CHAPTER XVIII

Miss Marcia's Story

EXULTING, THEY BUMPED ALONG THE ROAD UNTIL they reached Mike O'Brien and his bike. As had been prearranged, he had not entered the lonely road until he saw the mayor's car leave it. So he had waited on the corner of the avenue until the coast was clear.

Harry stopped beside him. "Anything to report, son?"

"Yes, sir," the freckled-faced boy replied. "I did just like you said. I hid my bike and the paper bag in the bushes and climbed a tree. I climbed up real high, so I could see around the bend." He patted the small binoculars which hung from a strap around his neck. "I got these with box tops, so I brought 'em along. They're not so hot, but I could see better than I could've without 'em. And just like you said, along 'bout six o'clock I see the mayor's big red sedan come around the bend and park over on one side. Pretty soon a taxi comes from the other direction and stops beside him. The driver reaches out of the window and the mayor hands him something. Couldn't see what it was, but it wasn't very big. Then the taxi backs and turns and drives off. The mayor does likewise. What cooks, Harry?"

"Can't tell you now, Tommy," Harry said. "But you'll find out soon enough. Many thanks. You're a great little detective."

"He certainly is," Cherry agreed as they turned into the broad avenue. "Did you tell him to climb a tree?"

"Only with the idea of making sure that the mayor couldn't see him," Harry admitted. "I didn't ask him to do any spying on the rendezvous, but I might have known he would. All kids his age are embryo FBI agents."

"He'll make a good witness if we need him," Cherry added. "There can't be any doubt now that Huey is blackmailing Mr. Hillman."

"The only way we can prove it," Harry pointed out, "is for one or both of them to confess. But if things get too hot around here for the mayor, he'll abscond, decamp, abdicate—or whatever you want to call it. And that, in view of the charges I'm going to make publicly, will amount to the same thing as a confession."

"What if he turns around and sues you for libel instead?" Cherry asked anxiously.

Harry shrugged. "I'm willing to take that chance. Any risk is worth while if it'll wake up this town to what's going on—and more especially, to what went on twenty-five years ago."

Suddenly Cherry made up her mind. "Take me

straight to The Manor, Harry. It's a little late for tea, but I'm going to try to see Miss Marcia right away and tell her everything."

Ten minutes later she was seated in front of the blue-tiled fireplace in Miss Marcia's lovely early American living room. "And now, my dear," Miss Marcia said gently, "you were going to tell me something which you felt was vitally important?'

Cherry clasped her hands, tongue-tied with embarrassment. Dr. Clem hadn't wanted to discuss the accident and she felt sure that Miss Marcia would feel even more strongly about it. Where should she begin the story? Finally she blurted:

"What would you think, Miss Marcia, if I told you that Mayor Hillman was being blackmailed by Turner Huland?"

Miss Marcia's black eyes were round with surprise. "Turner Huland," she repeated slowly. "Why, it was he —he, who—who—"

Cherry nodded encouragingly. "I think Mr. Hillman bribed him to say what he did. And I think that he's been blackmailing Mr. Hillman ever since."

Miss Marcia stiffened. "I don't want to talk about the accident. I don't want to think about it. It was so horrible. I was deliriously happy, singing to myself, when those headlights came around the bend. They blinded me, and—and that's all I remember."

"But were you really and truly driving too fast?" Cherry prodded gently. "Because I don't think you were. It's a known fact that Mr. Hillman always drives too fast. I think he forced you off the road and bribed Huey Huland to lie to the police."

"But he saved my life," Miss Marcia protested. "The doctors said so. An artery in my leg was severed when I was thrown through the windshield. That's what they told me when I regained consciousness."

"And so they made a hero of him," Cherry said flatly. "The only reason why he applied that tourniquet is because he's not a murderer!"

Miss Marcia stood up and her lips were gray. "I won't discuss the matter any further unless you can provide me with proof of your implications."

Cherry stood up too. "I know for a fact," she said determinedly, "that Mr. Hillman and Mr. Huland meet at the same hour on the first day of every month at a lonely spot on Bullethole Road. Why do they meet secretly? And what happens to the funds which the town allocates to the mayor for improving and maintaining the tenements?"

Miss Marcia began to talk then, more to herself than to Cherry. "I remember distinctly that I shifted into second in order to make the hairpin turn safely, and because the next bend comes so soon after the first, I continued in second gear." As she talked on and on, Cherry gathered that Miss Marcia had been blinded by the headlights of the other car, so she had no idea whether the driver was going too fast or not.

"But don't you see, Miss Marcia?" Cherry broke in. "If he had come around the bend slowly, there would have been plenty of time for both of you to stop. So he must have been driving too fast. You pulled over instinctively in order to avoid a head-on collision. That's why you ended up in the gully."

Miss Marcia shook her head. "It's too late to do anything now, so why discuss it?"

"It's not too late," Cherry protested. "Are you going to sit back and let that man be re-elected? Are you going to continue to let him pay off a blackmailer with town funds?"

"I certainly am not!" Miss Marcia came to life then and she moved swiftly across the room to the telephone. "I shall start out by notifying the *Sun* that I am definitely going to vote for Mr. Harry Jenner. Then I shall call every one of my old friends and repeat to them what you have told me. They can draw their own conclusions, but—"

"Every one of your old friends," Cherry interrupted softly. "And don't forget Dr. Clem. That's important. If *he* votes for Harry Jenner, it will surely mean a landslide election."

"Clem," Miss Marcia began and then abruptly changed the subject. "There's something I must explain to you now, Cherry. It's about the rebozo. Dr. Clem sent me one last Christmas, which looks exactly like yours. I told Mrs. Briggs to put it on a shelf in the upstairs hall closet. I never looked at it again until the night you arrived. I seldom go upstairs, you see. But that night I did and suddenly I wanted to see Clem's present. We would be celebrating our silver anniversary next month, you see. So I took the shawl down to my apart-

ment for a while and draped it around my shoulders
and—" Her voice ended in a sob.

"So that's who was crying that night," Cherry
thought. Aloud she said as she started for the door, "I
guessed that he gave you a rebozo like mine, but I *know*
that you are the only woman he could ever love. He told
me so himself." She slipped out into the hall and ran up
to her room.

As Cherry showered and got ready for her date with
Lex, she silently prayed that Miss Marcia would call
Dr. Clem. "If she does, he'll come right over no matter
what she says. I know he will. I know it." Then she began to worry, for fear he might be out on call. Miss
Marcia would never, never leave a message with the Answering Service. And she probably had no way of knowing that he didn't have office hours on Thursday evening.
Fretting, Cherry donned a pretty afternoon frock of pale-
blue taffeta and ran a comb through her dark curls.
Then she threw her coat over her shoulders and went
down to the East Parlor.

Lex was there and so was Harry, and they were glar-
ing at each other. Cherry was glad to see them both.

"Why don't you have dinner with us?" she asked
Harry. "I'm dying to hear the news and tell you mine."

Lex's temper flared, but before he could say a word,
Harry burst out with:

"My letter is going to be on the front page of tomorrow's *Sun*, Cherry. While I was there, Miss Marcia
called Bob Lindsay and told him that she was going to
vote for me. You could have knocked him over with a

feather. Reporters are scurrying all over town on foot and by phone to find out how many other old-timers have switched to me. That'll be a front-page story too, and the combination will spell r-u-i-n for His Honor."

"Politics," Lex said sulkily. "Why don't you go make speeches somewhere else?" Then he grinned. "Not that my opinion carries any weight, but I'm going to vote for you too. I saw those tenements last night, Cherry, and you're absolutely right. The mayor ought to be run out of town on a rail. I went to the health commissioner's office as soon as I got off duty this afternoon and who do you think was in the office making a report about the same matter?"

"Who?" Cherry asked curiously.

"Dr. Clem," he replied, "and was he wild! Seems he did some inspecting on his own after he left the Day Nursery and is he ever up in arms about the condition of those buildings! While I was there, the fire commissioner joined our little group, and when I left they were talking on the phone to the town supervisor. So I imagine there'll be another exciting front-page story in tomorrow's *Sun*."

Cherry sank down on a petit-point footstool. "It's too good to be true. Now if only we could get Dr. Clem and Miss Marcia together. Then we'd have a wedding, as well as a landslide election."

And then, as though in answer to her wish, she saw through the long window that Dr. Clem was lumbering up the front steps of The Manor as fast as he could!

CHAPTER XIX

Future Plans

AS HARRY HAD PREDICTED, THE FRONT-PAGE STORIES IN
Friday's *Sun* did spell ruin for Mayor Hillman. Cherry's
fears that he might turn around and sue Harry for libel
proved to be groundless. All that day reporters called by
phone and in person requesting an interview with His
Honor, so that he might refute the charges, but he had
his phone disconnected and refused to answer his doorbell.

Harry was not the only one who made campaign
speeches that day. In the morning Dr. Clem, Miss
Marcia, and Nellie Carson appeared on a local radio
broadcast stating vehemently that they were going to
vote for Harry Jenner. After that, several other influential citizens announced publicly that they too were
definitely "all out for Jenner."

Cherry spent the week end with the girls at No. 9,
and Harry met her at the station when she returned on
a Sunday evening train.

"Wait until you hear the latest news," he said as he helped her climb into his car. "I'm quite a little prophet in my own county, if I say so myself."

"But 'not without honor,' " Cherry quoted, "I hope."

"Not *His* Honor," Harry punned. "Listen. A committee of irate citizens, including the members of the town board, the police and fire and health commissioners, called upon him last night demanding that he appear publicly in answer to my charges. When he refused to answer the doorbell, they forced their way in and what do you think?"

Cherry sighed happily. "I can guess, without thinking, from the smug expression on your face. Instead of taking the risk of being run out of town on a rail, Mr. Hillman decided to run away under his own steam?"

Harry nodded and they drove off toward Main Street. "But right off he made the biggest mistake of his life. I guess he figured that he couldn't get far in that conspicuous maroon sedan of his, so he stole a jalopy from the used-car parking lot. Unfortunately for him, taking stolen property across a state line is a Federal offense, so even though he abandoned the jalopy in New Jersey and boarded a plane in Newark, he was picked up by FBI agents in Chicago early this morning."

Cherry sighed again, but not so happily. "Sending him to jail for stealing a car seems to me too mild a punishment for all of his crimes. Did I tell you that Miss Marcia's parents spent every penny they owned on her operations and treatments? When they died, she found that she didn't have a cent and that The Manor was mortgaged to the hilt. But she was fiercely determined to cling to the ancestral mansion and that's why she took in boarders. She couldn't have managed without Coombs and Mrs. Briggs who worked for free until the mortgage was paid off. I still think they're awfully sour, but I can't help admiring them for their loyalty."

"I agree," said Harry. "And now I can understand why Miss Marcia refused to marry Dr. Clem when she came back from Europe. He wasn't making enough money in those days to swing The Manor." He grinned ruefully. "The announcement of their wedding plans in yesterday's paper practically crowded me off the front page of the *Sun*. I saved some clippings for your scrapbook."

"Where will the bride and groom live?" Cherry asked curiously. "In his house or hers?"

"In his," Harry said with a chuckle. "The old couple will continue to run The Manor and keep the profits, just as though it belonged to them. Miss Marcia has left it to the Sleepyside Historical Society in her will, but the society can't inherit it until after Coombs and Mrs. Briggs pass on."

"That's a tidy arrangement," Cherry said. "I wish the mayor's ending could be so neat. And how about that blackmailer, Huey Huland? Is he going to get off scot free?"

"Hah!" Harry parked his car across the street from the coffee shop. "I shall tell you All over a piece of pie à la mode. Nobody is going to get off scot free or with a light sentence."

When they were settled comfortably in a booth inside the diner, Harry explained in detail:

"Before he decamped the 'Honorable' Cy left behind on his desk a full confession, implicating Huey Huland who was picked up late last night by a New York police detective and booked on an extortion charge. When confronted by the evidence we had gathered, plus Cy's confession, he admitted everything."

"But what on earth made Cy confess?" Cherry wanted to know.

Harry shrugged. "My theory is that he was sick and tired of being blackmailed and craved revenge. After all, the blackmailing had been going on ever since he was town supervisor. By the time he became mayor, his own funds were exhausted, and it was then that the town took over those tenements through tax liens. They were in good condition then and would have been sold quickly, but, according to his written confession, the mayor carefully squelched all prospective buyers. So the town, in order to get a return from the property, was virtually forced into the real-estate business, and through the passing of a referendum proposed by shrewd old Cy, the tenements became a town-operated housing project. As you know, the tenants stayed on and a large sum of money was allocated each year to the housing committee for the purpose of maintaining and improving the buildings. In a very short time the committee consisted of nobody but himself, and he wangled things so that he could operate the project without giving an accounting."

"He was a regular dictator, wasn't he?" Cherry asked.

"If only the town had elected Miss Nellie's husband as supervisor in the very beginning!"

"They could have avoided years of graft," Harry agreed. "But the present supervisor is a good man. The first thing he did, as acting mayor after reading Cy's confession, was to fire Mrs. Regan and hire a big husky man to take her place as the building's super. The Regans and Tim have been evicted. They have also been adopted. By Miss Nellie."

"How did she wangle that?" Cherry was surprised. "I thought they were all too proud to accept charity."

"It doesn't come under that heading," Harry said with a chuckle. "Leave it to Miss Nellie. She simply had them move bag and baggage to her house and they were too stunned to object until it was a *fait accompli*. Nellie and the acting mayor are as thick as thieves. She has already been appointed chairman of the housing committee. Workmen start tomorrow making improvements and repairs. She is going to supplement the fund with money of her own, and plans to have those tenements end up as model low-rent apartments. The street, at my suggestion, has been officially declared a park and is going to be converted into a private playground just for kids who live in the tenements. Deliveries and such will be made at the back entrances which open onto other, wider streets."

"Before you and Miss Nellie are through," said Cherry, "that will end up as the nicest part of town. Cy's arrest will surely mean that you will be unanimously elected."

"Not necessarily," he replied. "There are a few Rip Van Winkles in town who don't listen to the radio or read the paper. Between now and Tuesday evening when the polls close, I've got to go around and wake them up from their twenty-five-year nap. That is, if I want to be unanimously elected, and I do, because it will mean that the whole town has confidence in me and my program."

"I'll help," Cherry offered. "We are not going to have evening office hours on Tuesday."

So, although Election Day was a half holiday for Cherry, it was one of the busiest days of her life. From two until nine she and Harry called on the "Rips" and urged dozens of others to "get out and vote." When the polls closed, she and Harry went to the coffee shop for a late dinner, and it was there that he received the good news that he had been unanimously elected by a record number of voters. After Ben and Maria had congratulated him warmly, Harry and Cherry hurried off to The Manor to tell Miss Marcia and Dr. Clem the result of the election returns.

"This calls for a celebration!" Miss Marcia exclaimed. "I don't care if it is eleven o'clock."

She looked so young and beautiful as she called her friends that Cherry glowed with pleasure. Lex and Miss Nellie were among those invited to the cozy but gay party. At midnight the Answering Service called Dr. Clem. Cherry felt sure that he had been summoned to an emergency case, but when he placed the phone back in the cradle he was grinning broadly.

"'That," he said "was Lola, who, as I predicted, has changed her name to Barker. When the honeymoon is over, she is coming back to work for me. I have long needed two nurses," he added to Cherry.

Cherry grinned back at him. "No, you don't," she said firmly. "In the very beginning I guessed that Lola would get married and come back to you. It'll work out perfectly having the druggist's wife your office nurse. And I honestly don't think anybody could ever take Lola's place, Dr. Clem. She's your alter ego. And—surprise, surprise! I have another job waiting for me in Jamestown, Rhode Island."

Everyone stared at her in amazement, and Lex and Harry yelped in unison, "Oh, *no!*"

"Oh, *yes*," Cherry said laughingly.

Lex began to sulk but Harry asked curiously, "What kind of job is waiting for you?"

"I'm to be a boarding school nurse," Cherry told him cheerfully. "While I was at No. 9 Sunday afternoon my mother called me in answer to my last letter. The very fashionable Jamestown Academy is in desperate need of an R.N. The head nurse of the infirmary wants to take a long leave of absence to visit her folks in Ireland. The headmistress of the academy went to school with mother and so she wrote her asking if I was available." She turned to Dr. Clem. "Which I am now, am I not, sir?"

He fondly patted her hand. "You may leave in time to spend the Thanksgiving holidays at home. I'll miss you. We *all* will."

"We certainly will," the others chorused.

Lex recovered from his sulks long enough to mutter darkly, "Here today and gone tomorrow. That's Ames for you.

Harry glared at him. "Don't tell *me* your troubles. Nobody is going to miss Ames more than I will. If it hadn't been for her, I would never have been elected!"

Cherry smiled at them both and said softly, "Sleepy-side-on-Hudson is one of the nicest towns in the world, but there's no place like Hilton, Illinois!"